Time and Chance, An Iowa Murder Mystery
Barbara Lounsberry, Editor
Gary Kelley, Illustrator
Amy Roach, Designer
Gregory Shanley, Project Director
Jons Olsson, Project Finance/Marketing Director

ISBN 0-9662041-1-5

Published by Public Radio KUNI

University of Northern Iowa
Cedar Falls, Iowa 50613-0359

TIME & CHANCE
AN IOWA MURDER MYSTERY

Edited by Barbara Lounsberry

CONTENTS

Acknowledgments

Public Radio KUNI's first book, *Moments In Iowa History*, published in 1997, was the result of a yearlong series for Iowa's Sesquicentennial. KUNI had broadcast short historical essays each weekday throughout 1996, Iowa's 150th year as a state. The response was so positive and the request for transcripts of these "Moments" so overwhelming, we decided to ask author Jean Florman to compile her series into book form. The broadcast series and the book were our way of helping with the sesquicentennial celebration.

Although this book is much different from *Moments in Iowa History*, it is similar in that it is part of a celebration. We are fortunate to live and work in a state where education is highly valued, where so many fine writers have practiced and continue to practice their craft. We decided to compile a list of excellent Iowa writers and ask them to participate in a chain novel. The idea was that each author would write a chapter to a novel that KUNI would publish. The only guidance they received was that the novel was to be a murder/mystery. There was no rough outline to follow. Each chapter was created based on the previous chapters.

Initially, I was concerned the authors might not want to put their professional reputations on the line. We were asking children's authors to write about murders, playwrights to create in novel form, and newspaper and magazine editors and columnists to write fiction. Fortunately, almost everyone loved the idea and wanted to participate. Only a handful of writers turned me down, and always because they were facing deadlines for other projects. Many of the writers who agreed also had other projects in the works, but decided to participate anyway. Thank you all!

KUNI wanted to do something drastically different for this second book, and we thought this would be a unique way to celebrate the wonderful writers who help make our lives full. The writers' decision to work on this strange project is a tribute to their creative spirits, and, in a sense, to KUNI. Almost without exception the writers said how much they enjoyed the station and that they would gladly help with what we hope will be a profitable fundraising project. We hope current and former KUNI staff members will feel proud and be pleased that their hard work is and has been appreciated.

In addition to the writers, I would like to thank University of Northern Iowa English Professor Barbara Lounsberry for naming the novel and titling most of its chapters and for continuity and copy editing of the text. This project turned out to be much more work for her than anyone anticipated, and she handled the workload with tremendous skill and good humor. She is a joy to work with. No wonder she is a part of just about every important committee formed at U.N.I.

Cedar Falls artist Gary Kelley continues to amaze us with his generosity. He and his lovely family have done so much for the station and community that it is almost impossible to thank them adequately. As everyone can see, Gary did his usual terrific work on the cover.

Our book designer, Amy Roach, has been a great help in leading us through the world of publishing. We learned a great deal publishing *Moments In Iowa History*, but we are far from experts. The book looks great, and that is directly due to Amy.

KUNI thanks Humanities Iowa for assistance with authorship funding. KUNI also thanks the University of Northern Iowa Graduate College for providing a grant to help fund this book.

This volume is the result of hard work by the entire staff at KUNI. Special mention should be made of KUNI Development Director Jons Olsson. The magic he is able to perform behind the scenes with budgets and grant writing helps ensure the success of many station projects.

I cannot help but wonder if a book has ever been put together quite like this one. From the time the boss gave the go ahead for the book until it was printed none of the principals met face to face. The work was accomplished almost entirely by telephone and e-mail. The authors agreed by phone to do the project. I e-mailed them chapters as they came in, so those who wrote later did not have to read everything at the last minute. When a new chapter was due, it was e-mailed to me. I forwarded it to Barbara Lounsberry for editing. She sent it back to me and I sent it to our book designer Amy Roach. Amy produced the layout and mailed the chapters back to me; I mailed them to the authors for one last look and they sent their chapters back to me. Then, I left these chapters in the door at Barbara's house. She looked at the changes the authors suggested for their chapters, okayed them, added some finetuning of her own, and got them back to me. I mailed this final copy back to Amy to make the necessary changes! That process basically helped create this book from inception to printing in about six months.

The Iowa murder mystery you are about to read and its characters are totally fictitious. Any similarity to real people or actual events is strictly coincidental. Our authors have created colorful characters, and some of them (naturally) use colorful language. This book in no way represents the opinions of staff members of KUNI or the University of Northern Iowa.

Greg Shanley
Project Director
KUNI News Director

The race is not to the swift, nor the battle to the strong, nor bread to the wise, nor riches to the intelligent, nor favor to the skillful; but time and chance happen to all.

Ecclesiastes 9:1

1

Determinedly Picturesque

by Rebecca Christian

Monday, April 1

Being owner of the Three Sisters Bed and Breakfast Inn was glamorous, Charlie decided, as long as you didn't mind getting up at the dawn's early light to whip up Belgian waffles, sharing your bathroom with eccentric strangers and not having enough money to pay the light bill.

Charlie shivered. She flipped the radio on just as an apologetic announcer warned that icy roads and dense patches of fog in rural areas were not an April Fool's Day joke; school buses would run an hour late today. Wisps of fog showed through the kitchen windows, which were etched with frost.

Looking through them, Charlie could glimpse the swiftly flowing coffee-colored water of the Mississippi River a half a mile distant, and the gray, blurred shapes of the surrounding bluffs.

Even for Iowa, it had been a freakish March. During unseasonably warm weather the last couple of weeks, the tender shoots of crocuses along the veranda were peaking up through the thawing soil. She hoped they would be okay.

Charlie put the French roast beans in the coffee grinder, then snipped herbs into an egg mixture that was going to become a frittata. Next, she took after the eggs a bit more briskly than was necessary with a wire whisk. Her soon to be ex-husband Spence could always talk her into anything. Even as she slaved away in the kitchen this morning, he was upstairs sleeping peacefully as a newborn under the feather ticking in the Gentleman's Chamber. Their Boston bulldog terrier, Margaret, would normally be down here begging by now. Today, no doubt, she was waiting patiently at the foot of her sometime lord and master's fourposter bed.

"Can't we be civilized, love?" Spence had asked in the foyer late last night, making Charlie feel petty in spite of herself. When he showed up unexpectedly, she suggested he stay at the Slumberama Motel across the river in Vermillion Falls, Wisconsin. In the determinedly picturesque Iowa town of Bella, where Charlie's bed and breakfast was located, the dozen old inns were at full occupancy. Due to strict zoning laws that kept the Civil War-era look of the town pristine for the tourists, there was not a single modern motel inside the city limits.

"Well, we have one room left," Charlie muttered ungraciously, "but you'll have to pay like everyone else."

Spence tilted her chin up and she thought she could almost read regret in his eyes.

"I have been paying, Charlotte, ever since I left." He was the only person who ever called her Charlotte, so delighted was he by the notion that her English teacher mother had named Charlie and her two sisters after the Brontes. Sheesh, how could she still fall for his tricks and feints?

The familiar sound of a smoker's cough in the kitchen doorway interrupted her thoughts. Charlie turned and smiled. Her friend and assistant inn-keeper, Dixie, was up and no doubt desperate for the first of many Cokes of the day.

15

"Morning, Dix."

"Don't start with me."

Dixie foraged in the refrigerator and flipped the top of a Coke can with an expert, lacquered talon. She took a long pull. Her contacts weren't in yet, and she peered farsightedly into a buttered casse-role as Charlie put the egg mixture into it.

"What's all this green stuff?"

"Chives," Charlie frowned, realizing she really had overdone it. "A powdered sugar donut and a can of caffeine aren't everybody's idea of the most impor-tant meal of the day. How was your date with the living dead?"

Dixie, who was forty something, 20 pounds over-weight and seven times a grandma, always had at least one man panting after her. This month's ro-mance had started when Dr. Henry Maguire ventured gingerly into Dixie's beauty parlor to have the fringe around his balding pate trimmed when his own bar-ber went on vacation. Putting him at ease, Dix al-lowed as how she had always found older, balding men attractive (never mind that she found young men with full heads of hair and most men in between attractive, too). Dr. Maguire was in late middle age and so solitary and confirmed a bachelor that there had always been whispered speculation in Bella that he was gay.

"No sir," Dixie assured Charlie after their first few dates. "We went to the roadhouse in Vermillion Falls and did the country two-step."

Dixie described last night's interlude, sucking a Coke with one hand and grasping a countertop for support with her other. She was not a morning person.

"Dr. Maguire does the country two-step?" Charlie asked.

"Sure. Anyhoo, it beats staying home and watching *Green Acres* with you. What have we got today, all boat people?"

Boat people were not refugees, but the gambling enthusiasts who were flocking into Bella. Lately the little town had been a hotbed of controversy. Bella, population 3,997, was a quaint town halfway between Des Moines and Chicago that let hordes of tourists from both cities all think it was their own private discovery. A few months ago, a group of Des Moines developers who had long smelled money in the idea of operating a floating casino in the already wildly popular tourist town, had finally succeeded in securing a license.

Rabid opposition to the gambling boat had come from several sources. The most strident was Pastor Paula Swenson's antigambling group, who opposed it on religious grounds. Another source of opposition was a group of old-line, old money residents who feared that a ticky-tacky atmosphere, complete with the horrors of go-carts and t-shirt shops, would envelope their carefully preserved Victorian oasis. And, of course, there were the fierce environmentalists who were bent on protecting the wildlife in an inlet that had to be dredged so the boat could dock.   *17*

In the end, local greed and the tactics of rich developers from Des Moines prevailed. It seemed to Charlie that the tide began to turn when developers brought in Paddy Murphy, a flamboyant local businessman. Paddy ran the Murphy Stagecoach Stop, a century old inn. In a bit of sleight of hand that Charlie suspected was Spence's, the development corporation named Paddy president. This put the boat business over the top by making it look more like the product of good old homegrown enterprise than an exploitative scheme by greedy outsiders. After much strife, the county supervisors voted to let the boat come in and agreed to finance improvements to the harbor where it would dock.

"This here's a cash cow for the county," was the way County Supervisor Floyd Delmer, who farmed 500 acres just west of Bella, put it. "Let's get out to the barn and start milking."

Charlie could always count on Floyd for a good earthy quote. In addition to covering county news for the local twice weekly paper, *The Bella Whig*, Charlie had just started correspondent work for the *Des Moines Register* a few weeks before. Her favorite professor from journalism school at Iowa State, Wild Bill Watson, had tired of academia and was back in the trenches, working as a state editor there. Enough

Iowans either vacationed in Bella or had second homes there that its happenings were of interest to readers of the statewide paper. Between the boat and the protesters, Bella was potentially a big story these days, and Charlie knew that Bill was taking a chance on her. She wasn't about to let him down.

And so Charlie was on hand last week when the floating casino *La Bella*, a modern yacht disguised with a fake paddlewheel and a decorating scheme Charlie thought of as Victorian bordello by Disney, glided into the harbor. Cruising calmly at twelve knots, she journeyed up to Bella from the boatyards in Florida where she was built. Up she sailed through the Gulf of Mexico, faux crystal chandelier prisms trembling in anticipation. Last week she had slipped quietly into her dock in Bella Lake, an inlet of the Mississippi River that was tranquil as a farm pond but fed eventually into the river's turbulent main channel. Then all hell broke loose.

Environmentalists paraded around the harbor with dead carp; Pastor Paula's group picketed, praying, and impossibly thin and well-dressed network television reporters gave tiny Bella flattering national attention. The floating casino was scheduled to set sail on her maiden voyage on April 1, an irony that was not lost on the protesters. As a result, Charlie's inn, the Three Sisters, was enjoying better midweek occupancy than it had during its entire first year of operation.

"Who all is bellying up to the trough this morning?" Dixie asked Charlie as the two got the breakfast preparations underway.

"Let's see."

Charlie, who was 5 feet, two inches, on tiptoe, dragged a step stool over to a high cupboard and felt blindly for fluted champagne glasses for mimosas, a mix of champagne and orange juice that she ordinarily served only on weekends. It seemed to strike just the right note for this morning, however, the festive day of *La Bella's* maiden voyage. She ticked off a guest list for Dix.

"Ken, the Japanese TV producer, is still here. I switched Lawrence Thomas, that nice man from the La Bella corporation, to the Captain's Quarters because he needs his own phone. Doris and Mary Lou, the gambling fanatic sisters you met yesterday, are in Isabella's room—and Spence blew in last night."

"Spence!" Dixie crumpled her Coke can in one hand and slam dunked it into the bin for returns. "That explains the chives. The jerk still makes you nervous. Why didn't you tell him they were keeping the light on for him at the Bates Motel?"

"He pays the mortgage on this money pit, remember?"

"So?" Dix shrugged. "He owes you that much, big time."

"So, let's talk about something else. Can you cover for me today?"

"Guess so," Dixie sighed. "I gotta perm Poor Ellen Gutcheon at 11:30 but her hair's so thin it shouldn't take long. What's up?" Dixie always referred to Ellen as if "Poor" was her first name.

"The cruise is at one. I want to get out there good and early to make sure I get on the boat."

"Brenda Starr," Dixie teased. She pulled a cutting board out from a slot under the counter and started hacking kiwi for fruit cup with a butcher knife; the Coke had kicked in.

"Could be an interesting day," Charlie said.

"Betcha Pastor Paula's gonna pitch another hissy fit, especially with all the reporters around," Dixie speculated.

"Most likely. She stopped here last night to tell Lawrence Thomas she was going to get an injunction against the boat setting sail today."

"You know Paula," Dixie rolled her eyes. "Probably hot air."

"Probably," Charlie agreed as she tucked an embroidered napkin around a pair of croissants in a small wicker basket and arranged it next to a pot of Earl Grey tea on a lacquered tray. Very pretty. Nobody would be able to tell she'd gotten all of these fine family heirlooms at garage sales.

"Could you take this up and put it outside Lawrence's door?" she asked Dix.

"So early?" Dix asked.

"He wanted to go birdwatching this morning before we serve."

Dixie made a face.

"I didn't think he was the type."

Lawrence Thomas' request for an early breakfast basket had surprised Charlie, too. He was a big bear of a man with a sardonic manner, lambent eyes, a little paunch he patted as if it were a pet, and a neatly trimmed black beard just beginning to go gray. All of her other birder guests had been wiry and aggressively fit. Dix, of course, thought all birdwatchers were sissies. Ironically for an innkeeper's assistant, her idea of classy accommodations was a Holiday Inn where the water pressure flattened her against the shower wall, the bed had Magic Fingers, and room service stayed open all night.

What would she do without Dixie? Charlie wondered. Things had fallen apart for both of them a year ago. First Spence came in from a jog one morning and announced that he still loved Charlie but wasn't sure if he wanted to be married anymore. Shortly thereafter, Dixie's fourth husband, a semi-driver, took up with the waitress at the truck stop where he always stopped for a hot beef sandwich in western Nebraska.

"I dunno, Charlie," Dix had mused as they commiserated at the roadhouse in Vermillion Falls.

"Me neither, Dix."

Charlie, who could get drunk sniffing a cork, toyed with a glass of Lambrusco. Dixie was wearing one of her several pairs of violently tinted contacts and her aquamarine eyes were unfocused as she drank directly from a pitcher of strawberry daiquiris.

"Maybe your next hubby should have a name that starts with a letter besides 'D,'" Charlie suggested helpfully.

Dixie's husbands were, in order, Delbert, Dwayne, Darryl and Dewey. The only one she had a soft spot for was Delbert, who married her when she was 16 and rescued her from a hard scrabble life as the oldest of ten feisty kids on a little farm in the "boot" of southern Missouri. She still called Delbert once a

21

year on their anniversary to say it sure had been fun while it lasted. To avoid confusion, she referred to the husbands that followed generically as Dick—handy, she said, because it was also short for "Dickhead."

22   Dixie had shaken her head mournfully at Charlie's suggestion that she venture further down the alphabet.

"That wouldn't help. With me, Charlie, marriage is like a bad perm—it never seems to take."

So far, Dix and Charlie's arrangement was working out better than either of their marriages had. Even with Spence paying the mortgage, Charlie hadn't been able to keep her combined income from the inn guests and her fledgling free-lance writing attempts steady enough to keep up with the bills. And the overhead had been killing Dixie in her beauty shop, where she and Charlie got acquainted when Charlie first moved to Bella. (A true test came when Dix tried to do "something real clever" with Charlie's long and unruly dark hair. Their fledgling friendship survived the experiment even though Charlie had to wear her black bowler hat most of the time for a while.)

After they both shipwrecked on the high seas of marital misadventure, the unlikely friends decided to pool resources. Dixie moved into the Three Sisters Inn and opened a two-chair salon in what had been the cellar keeping room of the Queen Ann mansion that Charlie was still in the process of restoring. She named the shop "Dixie's Keeping Room: Keeping You Beautiful." They shared the tasks of tending the inn and its guests. Each laid claim to one of the tiny maids' rooms for her own.

As the still wintry sun rose reluctantly in the sky outside, Charlie finished setting the table. It was eight by the time guests Doris and Mary Lou appeared in the kitchen doorway, demonstrating identical Queen of Hearts sweatshirts—the crowns lit up with miniature Christmas tree lights when they pushed buttons in the sleeve. Dixie woo-wooed.

"Looks like you're all ready for the cruise. How about some coffee?" Charlie asked.

"We thought you'd never ask," Doris tittered. The sisters were having a giddy rendezvous away from the objects of much merriment, their pesky, retiree husbands, identified only as Himself (Doris' husband) and The King (Mary Lou's). Charlie wondered what their lives were like at home—she hoped not too dreary.

Doris and Mary Lou were followed closely by Spence and his adoring canine pal, Margaret, her toenails clicking on the kitchen's terra cotta floor.

The kitchen was getting crowded. It wasn't as spacious as visitors assumed it would be from seeing the other rooms. Trust the selfish old Victorians to give themselves boudoirs the size of ballrooms and stiff the cook on space, Charlie thought sourly.

Margaret pawed at Charlie's hem, looking up at her with froggy, supplicating eyes. Charlie, whose hands were full of silverware, turned to Spence.

"Would you let her out, please?"

Spence pouted a little as he removed the brick from the kitchen door that wouldn't stay shut, giving

Charlie a look that asked: Who, me? Do something besides keep you off balance?

Maybe it was a good thing that their attempts to have a baby failed, Charlie thought sadly. Spence changing a diaper would have been on par with the Prince of Wales pumping his own petrol. Spence had moved back to his family's Des Moines law firm, Wood and Wood, when he left the Three Sisters Inn in Charlie's shaking hands. His Bella connections still came in handy, as the addition of the La Bella developers to his list of high-powered clients proved. Since he was a former Bella resident, the Des Moines based developers used him as a sort of liaison between the local yokels and the city boys. His work with the boat company was the reason he was in town now; keeping Charlie on an emotional rollercoaster was just a fringe benefit. He was criminally handsome today in a charcoal suit with one of the blindingly white shirts Charlie used to take to the cleaners for him, heavy starch.

While a persnickety Margaret searched for the ideal place to do her business in the yard, Spence leaned against the doorway and chatted up "the girls" on the virtues of roulette over craps.

"The odds are heartless," he shrugged, "but it's so elegant who could resist?"

Not Doris and Mary Lou, apparently, although Charlie was willing to bet they had never played anything but the slot machines in their long lives.

Charlie suppressed a groan. It never failed. Spence was a man of many gifts. He could coax a roaring fire out of two green twigs and a soggy match, go into any city and drive unerringly to the best Italian restaurant, discuss the Irish poets as easily as the NBA playoffs. But by far his greatest talent was his ability to divine the secret vanity of any woman. Just now, Mary Lou's heavily ringed hands flew unconsciously up to the blue helmet of her hair. Doris gazed raptly at Spence as she smoothed her knit pants over her wizened behind.

Meanwhile, Margaret the bulldog was outside, whining piteously. (Spence, of course, had forgotten he let her out). Charlie opened the door for her and gave her a conciliatory pat. The beast couldn't help herself. Spence worked the same magic on all the ladies—except Dixie, who had her contacts in now and was taking his measure through narrowed, unnaturally lavender eyes.

Finally, the hash browns were crisp enough and the last guest, Ken Wakabayashi, made his way down to the dining room to read the papers. He gave short shrift to the *Chicago Tribune* and *Des Moines Register* but studied the *Bella Whig's* obituaries and school lunch menus as avidly as Margaret Mead observing the rituals of the Samoans.

"Tater tot casserole and peach crisp at the junior high today," he told Charlie.

"Tasty." Charlie, who was carrying the frittata to the table, rubbed her stomach with her free hand.

"Services for Ethel Holmrickhausen of Luther Manor on Saturday. Visitation after 7 tonight at the Schwiegart Brothers Funeral Home. Do you suppose it will be an open casket?" Ken asked eagerly. Midwestern funeral customs mesmerized him.

"I know it will be," Dixie answered. "I did her hair last night. It was just like yours, Charlie, strong as baling wire."

"Thanks for sharing that, Dix," Charlie said. Charlie was relieved that Ken didn't mention the article she wrote about Pastor Paula's protest at the County Board of Supervisors meeting; she'd already heard enough about that when Frank Gleason, the attorney for the supervisors, called to complain last night. It was a delicate enterprise, covering the news in a place where you also lived and tried to run a business. And she certainly didn't want to discuss the article with Spence, who had said rather righteously that he considered it a conflict of interest for her to report on a business in which her husband was involved as an attorney, even if they weren't living together anymore.

"Come and get it!" Dixie ballyhooed, more chuckwagon master than innkeeper as she herded the other guests from the kitchen to the dining room.

Charlie felt silly treating her husband as a guest while he bantered with the ladies. It made her grateful for the presence of Ken. The Japanese film director had been staying for two weeks already, making a documentary on what he cynically called "The Wholesome American Heartland" for Tokyo television. Not only was his long stay helping her cashflow, but Charlie enjoyed the relish with which Ken bashed stereotypes about the Japanese. He carried a camera only when filming, and he was far from elaborately polite. In fact, he could be downright irascible, instructing the others to call him Ken because he couldn't stand the way Americans pronounced his Japanese name. He had gone to graduate school in New York City and his English had a style all its own—slightly accented and highly colloquial.

"Here's your fruit cup, whatsyourname," Charlie told him.

"What?" Ken asked. "No sushi? You can call me Elvis today."

Charlie was itching to know Ken's real first name, but his refusal to tell her had become a game between them.

"What's all this green?" he asked, poking suspiciously at his serving of frittata.

Dixie, who was dealing out apple walnut muffins like a card shark, caught Charlie's eye and raised one of her vigorously plucked brows.

"Chives," Charlie answered Ken. "Don't you grow herbs in the mysterious Far East?"

"Just ginseng. Never chives."

"I thought ginseng was from China."

"China, Japan, what's the difference?" Ken slathered his hash browns with ketchup.

Spence speared a fresh pineapple chunk with the faintly injured air of someone who thought he had an exclusive franchise on repartee. Ken looked from Spence to Charlie with frank curiosity, sensing the tension. Charlie suspected he was a very good journalist.

Rebecca Christian is a native Iowan (born and raised in Des Moines, where she now lives), and a graduate from the journalism school at Iowa State University. She is an essayist, travel writer and playwright. She writes a regular weekly column for the Telegraph Herald *in Dubuque, is a correspondent for the* Des Moines Register, *and often writes about Iowa for national and regional magazines.*

Several of her plays have Iowa characters or settings, including First Lady Lou *(about Lou Hoover, performed at the Smithsonian),* Chief, A Terrible Stillness, Insomniacs, Just Suppose *(all as a solo author) and* Dear Iowa *(a collaboration with several writers and musicians, including Mary Swander).*

Her new play, Mothering Heights, *is a musical comedy revue written in collaboration with composer Tracy Rush.*

2

Mississippi Bluff

by Dan Weeks

"I AM a very good journalist," said Ken matter-of-factly. He was looking straight at Charlie, smiling faintly, fork still in hand.

Charlie paled, then reddened. She whirled around and headed for the sink, grabbed a dishrag, and started wiping the counter with a sort of frantic aimlessness, a panicked, puzzled look on her face. She was either losing her sanity, saying things she'd sworn she'd just thought, or Ken could read minds.

"Never said you weren't," muttered Spence reflexively, popping the pineapple chunk into his mouth.

Charlie was instantly incensed by Spence's response. How typical! How infuriatingly, characteristically egotistical of the man to assume Ken was responding to HIM!

Of course, Charlie's thoughts continued, since Ken was male and world-traveled, Spence was agreeing with him, or at least not disagreeing. If SHE had said Ken was a good journalist, Spence would have challenged, discounted, and suavely belittled her for the thought.

For some reason, the knowledge that it was her THOUGHT that Spence was responding to, and that he was responding completely DIFFERENTLY to it because he didn't think it was hers drove her right over the edge. It took her just a split second to go from private, simmering, self-righteous victimhood to public rage.

"No, you didn't," she exploded, whirling to face Spence. "But if I had said it, you'd have wanted PROOF!" She smacked her wet dishrag on the cutting board she had been wiping, wishing she was holding something more substantial. Her Chinese chopper, for instance. She imagined the force of her knife blow neatly splitting the board in two, sending a fist-sized chunk of end-grain rock maple spinning towards Spence's neatly combed head.

Spence started. He stopped mid-chew. He gazed in amazement at Charlie. "I simply agreed . . . ," he began.

"NO. You did not SIMPLY AGREE. You just didn't DISAGREE. With HIM." Charlie pointed at Ken.

She was trembling, unstoppable. She realized she was about to go off on a raging monologue, a *non sequitur* of a tirade that no one else in the room would understand. But she could NOT ABIDE the idea that Spence had somehow managed to show up in HER kitchen, just in time to edit, by implication, HER very thoughts about the most interesting guest she'd had since opening and of whom, she realized in one of her characteristic run-on thoughts, she was feeling rather fond. And, having the rapt attention of everyone in a room, perhaps for the first time in her life, she wasn't about to stop.

"With ME, you would have disagreed," she continued, still shaking, voice clenched and quavering. "You would have said I didn't have enough EVI-DENCE (she smacked the cutting board again with her dishrag). That I was ROMANTICIZING. (Smack!) I never said he WAS a good journalist! DAMN IT. (Smack!) I said I SUSPECTED he was a good journalist!"

"I said I was a good journalist," Ken corrected her. "YOU didn't say anything."

"Oh GOD!" said Charlie, now more exasperated than unsettled. "YOU'RE no help at all! That's not my point! My point is that HE," she pointed again, District-Attorney-in-the-courtroom-style, at Spence, "HE has come back to ruin my life by undermining my confidence just when I thought I was rid of him! New business, exotic guests, big things happening in town and me getting to take part, and now Spence gallops in—and I let him edit my very thoughts."

She paused to inhale. No one moved. Ken's feint smile hung in the air like the Cheshire cat's. Dixie seemed as though she was about to move closer to Charlie as a show of sisterly solidarity, but decided simply to flash her a "You go, girl!" look instead.

Meanwhile, Spence was trying hard to appear un-ruffled, but his eyes darted from one guest to an-other, looking for a single trace of sympathy for him-self in the audience.

Charlie breathed deeply and increasingly calmly several times, reoxygenating, gathering strength for her finale.

"OUT!" she barked at Spence, with a vigorous, stiff-armed gesture at the door.

Spence blinked innocently, making one last attempt at the audience's good graces. "I just said . . ." he began, with an elaborate mildness he intended as charming, still glancing around furtively.

"OUT!"

Spence held up his hand in a gesture calculated to seem more considerate ("No need to go to further trouble on my account") than self-protective

"Just leaving," he said quietly. He glanced around once more for a murmur, a nod, a crack of sympathy showing in just one face, but even Doris and Mary Lou seemed transfixed by Charlie's performance.

"We're waiting," said Dixie sarcastically. Spence retreated to his guest room, trailing squeaky footsteps up the century-old staircase.

Would he leave, or had he just temporarily withdrawn? The unspoken question hung in the kitchen like the smell of breakfast. Coffee was stirred. The tablecloth was inspected. Ken raised the paper once again, and appeared to be reading it, though his ears seemed to stand at attention, as though listening for more creaks.

Charlie's adrenaline surge had crested, but still she carefully avoided picking up her Chinese chopper, hanging handily from the cupboard next to the sink, for fear of unintended consequences. Her shaking hands found a few more crumbs to sweep into the sink with her dishrag.

No one spoke until Spence descended again, moments later, and gingerly shut the front door behind him. There was a collective exhale.

"Is this the kind of Bed-and-Breakfast where

there's a play going on when you get there?" inquired Doris brightly. "Right around you? A friend in my bridge club said a guest was poisoned at the dinner table at The Manse-on-the-Mound in Dubuque. She hadn't read the brochure and had no idea! The dead guest got up again at the end of the scene, of course, and everybody clapped."

33

Dixie took the cue and smacked her hands together *con vivace*. "Good show!" she said, with a broad wink at her friend and business partner. The rest of the guests caught on. Even Ken put down his paper and joined in.

"A curious custom, these dramas," he said knowingly as the applause died off, still grinning faintly. "It hasn't yet caught on in Japan.

"But since it's from the West," he continued, with what Charlie thought was just a trace of sarcasm, "I don't see why it wouldn't. You and Spence should come over. Give it a try! You'd make a fortune in yen. Then you could come back here and really— go to town—right?—with this place. Import all your Japanese customers. Buy the gambling boat. Buy every old inn here, perform a different mystery in each one! Disneyland on Mississippi for Japanese tourists! Take my advice," he said, getting up from the table, again looking Charlie straight in the eye, again with that feint smile, "and you will be rich.

"Such talent should not be wasted," he added. He winked at Charlie, neatly folded the paper, and padded off to his room to brush his teeth.

"It's about time someone nailed that fancy-pants ex-husband of yours," chortled Dixie after Doris and

Mary Lou had also left the table. She and Charlie were in the kitchen, cleaning up. "First time I've seen HIM speechless."

"Soon-to-be ex-husband," Charlie reminded her absently, sudsing a plate with one of those dish scrubbers that looks like a long-stemmed, ball-shaped flower with spiky foam-rubber petals.

"No, I think that did it," said Dixie, dishrag in hand. She'd been demoted from dishwasher-loader to plate-drier until they could get the aging Kitchenaid fixed.

"That's what the shrink that Dick and I went to called 'the moment of emotional divorce,'" she continued, wiping down forks with amazing speed and sending them clattering into the silverware drawer. "When you call it quits with the jerk in your heart. It's final, believe me. The rest is just paperwork."

"But how did he KNOW?" Charlie dropped her sudsy dishflower and turned to face Dixie.

"Because," said Dixie patiently, with the air of someone dealing kindly with the emotionally distressed, "you told him to leave. Twice. In no uncertain terms."

"Oh, yeah, him." Charlie brushed an unruly lock of hair from her eyes with a soapy hand. "I was thinking of Ken."

"From what I can tell, darlin'," said Dixie, "'Out!' is one of the several million English words Ken can understand."

"No," said Charlie. Now it was she that spoke patiently. "How did Ken know I suspected he was an excellent journalist? Did I say that?"

"Honey, you're lips were moving and words were coming out," said Dixie, starting on the butter knives. "I believe that's called talking in most parts of the world."

"No, no! I mean, did I say that THEN? That I thought Ken was a good journalist? When we were having breakfast?"

"How the HELL should I know? You said a lot of things. This morning nothing you said would surprise me. He looks like a good journalist to me. I went out with a reporter once. When he wasn't drinking or writing or snooping around, he was always reading the paper. Does Ken drink and snoop, too?"

"Oh, Dixie, I don't know. I hope not, at least not too much. He just seems like he knows what's going on, more than he appears to. For a minute there, I thought he could read my mind."

"Well, darlin'," said Dixie, raising her eyebrows suggestively, "maybe he can."

"Oh, stop it," said Charlie.

"But," she added with quiet determination, swabbing another plate, "I'm going to find out. Just you wait till dinner. I've got an idea."

Dan Weeks grew up in New England and came to Iowa in the mid-1970s to attend Grinnell College (B.A. American Studies) and the University of Iowa (M.A. Essay Writing). He has lived in Des Moines for the past 10 years with his wife, Deb Darge, and children, Abigail and Benjamin. During that time he has written and edited essays, features, and profiles for various magazines published by Meredith Corporation, including Traditional Home, Country Home, Better Homes and Gardens, *and* Northwest Airlines' World Traveler. *He is currently Managing Editor of Meredith's* Family Money *magazine. This is his first attempt at fiction.*

3

Personal Impact
by Venise Berry

Charlie's purple linen jacket flapped with determination as she trudged through the thick gust of
wind that assaulted her. She slid into the driver's
seat of her blue Chevy Prism and patted most of her
thick mane back in place. With breakfast over and
Spence out of the way, at least for a while, she could
focus on her next story.

She pushed the key into the silver ignition and
listened to the rebuilt engine whirl. What was it
about that man that made her crazy inside? Now
she felt bad about her outburst this morning, but
that was the nature of their entire three years together. Being with Spence was like riding the twirl-
ing teacups at Six Flags complete with hard, uncom-
fortable seats, limiting attachments, and moments
of heart pounding, dizzying emotion.

She checked her watch. The gold Timex had been
with her longer than any man. It was almost 9:30.
Charlie had about an hour to gather what she needed
before she'd have to rush back and prepare a light
lunch for her guests. She had already organized most
of the ingredients for her wild mushroom soup and
spinach salad.

Releasing the emergency brake, Charlie backed out of the gravel driveway toward the street. As she twisted her head around to the left to get a better view, something darted past her peripheral vision off to the right. Before she could slam on brakes, she heard the thump of her bumper hitting it.

Charlie jerked her head right, then left, but saw nothing moving except the fledgling leaves on a nearby bush that defied the wind's effort to carry them away. She hopped out of the car and searched the ground. Nothing. Only traces of wetness lingered from the morning's icy surprise. She looked out across the heavily wooded lot next to her inn, then over the grassy field behind, but there was no sign of the possible victim.

Maybe it was a dog, she thought as she walked back to the car and opened the door. Paddy Murphy's pompous mutt ran around town all the time without a leash. Just yesterday he had stopped to shit in her yard right in front of her without fear, practically daring her to do something about it. And when he was finished, she swore he threw his long nose up into the air and moved his four legs past her with the same arrogant strut of his master.

Charlie got back into the car and slowly pulled out onto the narrow street. She turned her front wheels left and headed for the main library at Sycamore and Birch Boulevard. Additional statistics on gambling in the state was the first thing she needed to find. The next article in her series would look closely at the personal impact of gambling. It was another topic that Gleason would not be happy about. But as a journalist Charlie was obligated to present a balanced and accurate picture, and she, too, was good at what she did. She also remembered hearing something about the sale of the harbor several years ago that she wanted to check out. It was all fuzzy in her head now, but the implication she did remember was a negative one. Some kind of problem had emerged with the land, but was quickly dismissed or remedied.

If Charlie had looked back toward her combined home and place of business just before she turned the first corner, she would have seen Spence's car inch its way up against the curb across the street. He didn't get out right away. Just sat there with his windows cracked admiring the power of the sun as it warmed the cool breeze and lit the day brightly. Charlie was the only woman who had ever come close to understanding Spence. She somehow knew instinctively what he thought and how he felt. She could always see through his well prepared masks and was quick to make him take them off and deal with reality. She was as close to his soulmate as he would probably ever come.

So why couldn't he make the commitment she wanted? It wasn't another woman or anything like that. He had said "I do" with sincerity and had no desire to be with anybody else but Charlie in that way. He pondered his dilemma knowing deep down that his fears were responsible. His fear of imperfection. His fear of powerlessness. His fear of abandonment. There were others, but these three seemed to become overwhelming every time he let Charlie get

too close. He had spent most of his forty years con-
structing perfect masks for protection. He needed
his masks to conduct business and expand his social
circle. He needed his masks to keep his fears under
control.

40

"Hey! You okay?" Ken asked peering into the
driver's window of the car.

Spence jumped, not because of the intrusive voice
that interrupted his thoughts, but because of the
curious face that hovered within an inch of his own.

"Yeah. Just needed to get something out of the
house," Spence replied and quickly reached to open
the door.

Ken stepped back as the door swung open. "You
know that show, if that's what it was this morning,
would be a wonderful addition to my film project."

Spence hopped out of the car and grinned. "I doubt
if Charlie would want the Kodak moments between
us on tape, even in Japan."

Ken hesitated, then spoke. "Maybe you should
simply admit that you love her," he advised as if they
were old friends.

Spence curled the edges of his mouth upward. "If
it were that simple, we'd be up in the Gentleman's
Chamber right now," he bragged.

Ken nodded and added his own smirk. "The love
between men and women has no boundaries, my
mother said to me once. To be honest, I didn't inherit her optimism."

Why does this man feel the need to tell me about
his mother's optimism? Spence thought. He stood
and stared for a moment past Ken at a ground squir-

rel that had bolted up into the air on its hind legs not far away. "You don't need optimism in this country," Spence finally turned back to Ken and spit out. "Optimism only gets you kicked in the ass."

The library was a renovated old quilting factory. The one level, brick building held many shelves of mildewed treasures the librarian, Mrs. Pillsly, refused to throw away after the floods of 1993. She was a stereotypical librarian with long brown hair always tied into a neat bun on the top of her head, a narrow stick figure that dresses had difficulty clinging to and lips always pursed together in a prissy fashion. The only thing Mrs. Pillsly had done in her twenty-six years as the Bella librarian to update her look was buy a pair of gold, oval, wire-rimmed glasses with lenses that tinted automatically when she stepped into the sunlight.

"Charlie. You're my first patron today. Let me serve you," Mrs. Pillsly said with pride as Charlie entered.

"I need to get some current statistics on gambling in Iowa. You know, take a look at some of the things that have happened in other cities." Charlie went straight to the new computer reference system as she spoke. It had been donated and set up by La Bella Corporation last year during its negotiations with the City Council.

Charlie laughed as she clicked into the Internet system and typed in the key word gambling. She was probably one of the few people in town who could use the elaborate equipment. Although Mrs. Pillsly had attended several training sessions, she still had no real clue about the possibilities. She dutifully accepted the mass of modern machinery as a mysterious part of the family of knowledge she had vowed to protect.

"Mrs. Pillsly," Charlie called as she pushed the print button to copy several pages of information she'd found which might be useful.

Mrs. Pillsly appeared without a sound startling Charlie. "Can I help, dear?" she asked at the same time reaching up and straightening a leaning book on the shelf in front of her.

"Do you remember a few years ago when the harbor was sold?" Charlie asked, turning to give Mrs. Pillsly her full attention.

Mrs. Pillsly wrinkled her nose and ruffled her forehead intensely. "I remember the scandal about one of Pastor Swenson's deacons, brother Jonah I think they called him," Mrs. Pillsly explained as she pulled a book from another shelf, flipped it right side up and slipped it back into place. "His last name was Barnes or Burns, something like that. Anyway, this brother Jonah was caught taking money from the church. Rumors said it was more than a hundred thousand dollars over a bunch of years. And some of that money apparently ended up in the middle of that harbor deal."

Charlie shook her head and smiled. Mrs. Pillsly was always good for succulent tidbits of local gossip. Unfortunately it was just that— gossip. Charlie quickly discovered when she first began her writing career in Bella that although the gossip usually held a sliver of truth, the facts needed to be checked and rechecked, confirmed and reconfirmed.

"Is Jonah still living here?" Charlie asked and stood up to straighten her beige silk blouse.

"I haven't seen him in months, but his farm is about an hour away heading toward Des Moines, so he could still be around. If I remember right, they didn't press charges because some big muckity muck out of Des Moines was also part of the deal."

43

Charlie leaned forward and crossed her fingers. "Do you remember who it was?" she asked.

"I don't remember a name, but I bet Floyd would. He had just been elected County Supervisor when that stink erupted. It became a big mess and he had to deal with it."

"I think there was an article in the *Bella Whig* about it, could you find it for me, please?" Charlie raised her voice to a whiny tone for the word please and flashed her biggest smile to secure a positive response.

"You know I can't refuse you anything, Charlie," Mrs. Pillsly gave in and smacked her lips. "When do you need this article?"

"Before *La Bella* sails this afternoon," Charlie practically whispered.

Mrs. Billsly let out a deep breath, "I guess I should skip lunch, then."

Charlie hugged her tightly. "I'll bring you lunch. Wild mushroom soup and spinach salad," she said, then gathered her precious pages and darted out the double front doors. It was after 10:30, and she needed to get back to the inn.

In the meantime, Dixie was lifting the thin wisps of

dirty blonde hair that made up Poor Ellen Gutcheon's bangs. She patted and smoothed the gooey mixture with gloved hands carefully laying each strand back into the pile that collected at the top of Ellen's head.

"You think you'll be finished in time for me to watch Pastor Paula's bonfire?" Poor Ellen Gutcheon asked.

Dixie chuckled. Bella was truly a boring place when the most excitement they had had in a year was a burning pile of misplaced hope. "Sure, another five minutes and we'll be ready to rinse," she answered. "The set and dry shouldn't take more than thirty minutes."

As Dixie checked the cactus clock on the wall, a gift from her first husband on their honeymoon in Phoenix, she thought about how she had come to settle in Bella. Darryl Hamberg, her third husband had found the quaint little place on a fishing trip. He was adamant about moving to Bella from Chicago to secure his dreams of grandeur. Darryl was tired of being a little fish in a big pond. He wanted to try being a big fish in a little pond for a while. He planned to become Bella's premier jeweler with great prices and quality selection. After Christmas season when he realized that the money just wasn't there, his dream abruptly dissolved and he packed up heading back to Chicago.

Dixie had at first planned to go with him. At the time, Charlie was a new friend. They had only known each other for less than a month, but when the time came she couldn't leave. It was impossible to explain it to Darryl because she honestly didn't understand it herself. Somehow in Bella she had realized

Darryl's dream and become that big fish in the little pond. In Chicago, she was just one among many good hair stylists, but in Bella she was the Diva of hair. Some of her clients came from as far away as Des Moines and Davenport.

While she rinsed and set Poor Ellen Gutcheon's   45
hair she imagined all the things she could do to improve the woman's image. "You should let me color your hair next time Ellen. Believe me a bright firey red would give you such a glamorous look," Dixie teased.

"Mmmmmm," Ellen moaned her usual reply and nodded.

"Imagine your fire engine red hair scooped up on top of your head like so with a seductive curl just above you left eye," Dixie coaxed as she demonstrated in front of the mirror.

Ellen smiled at Dixie. She appreciated the potential for such excitement, but didn't think she could handle it.

"I wonder if it would make a difference?" Ellen would ask each week after soaking in Dixie's words.

"You'll never know unless you try," Dixie gave her the usual line, then gulped down the last of her third can of Coke.

Every week Dixie would go through her song and dance hoping to convince her favorite and most difficult client to take a chance and every week Ellen would walk out of the shop with that same hair in that same pageboy cut, loosely framing that same pale, oval face.

Charlie rushed home just in time to see Spence's tan Lexus pull away from the front of the house. She hesitated for a minute, then hurried inside to get lunch on the table. As she dropped the last of the mushrooms into the simmering pot, Doris and Mary Lou hustled in. They were even more excited about the trip because of rumors in town that Oprah Winfrey might make an appearance and invite some of the people on board to be guests on her show.

Lawrence Thomas from the La Bella Corporation was considerate enough to call and leave a message. He wouldn't make lunch. He was much too busy getting the final details in order for the ship's bon voyage.

Ken entered with his camera and a portable tape recorder slung over his shoulder. He carefully set the equipment down in the corner of the room and washed his hands in the sink. He had spent the morning interviewing and filming Pastor Paula's newest tirade near the dock. The tape rolled as her group joined with the environmentalists to create a modest pile of gambling paraphernalia and dead animals. The pile included a pool table, several Pokeno games, boxes of poker chips, lottery tickets, many dead fish, a smashed beaver, and hundreds of decks of cards. The symbolic bonfire of protest would take place at 1:00, the same time the ship was scheduled to sail.

Charlie set clean plates on the antique oak table, then tossed the spinach salad briskly in its glass bowl in the center. She pulled honey mustard, French, Italian and blue cheese dressings out of the refrigerator and placed them beside the salad in small bowls. Next, she filled each glass with fresh lemonade and served bowls of her award-winning wild mushroom soup. Charlie made sure each of her guests was satisfied before she hurried upstairs to gather her things for the trip.

Venise Berry is currently an Associate Professor at the University of Iowa in Journalism and Mass Communication. She grew up in Des Moines. She received her B.A. (Journalism) and M.A. (Communication Studies) from the University of Iowa in 1977 and 1979 respectively. In 1989, she earned her Ph.D. from the University of Texas in Austin. She has numerous scholarly publications to her credit, including her co-edited book, Mediated Messages and African American Culture: Contemporary Issues *(Sage, 1996) which won the Meyer Center award for the study of human rights in North America. Her first novel,* So Good *(Dutton/Penguin, 1996), was a Blackboard national bestseller and her second novel,* Serpentine Fire *(also Dutton/Penguin), will be released in 1999.*

4

In the Woods by the River

by Saul Shapiro

Eagles soared and tourists flocked. Life along the bluffs of the Mississippi River was idyllic for the nearly 4,000 residents of Bella, which swelled with visitors spring through fall. The town had managed to parlay the majesty of the Mississippi bluffs—including nearby Effigy Mounds National Monument and Pike's Peak State Park—with a robust antiques trade to keep local cash registers churning in the absence of any real industry.

Yet from Halloween, when the last tourist to leave town turned out all the lights, until mid-April, the silence was deafening and the business profits slowly declined. To entice the tourists, local business people dreamed up more festivities than Younkers has sales. Bella Barge Days, Lock and Dam Week, Flood of '93 Fest, and Fall Foliage Weekend merged seamlessly into an ongoing party for the nature lovers and antiques enthusiasts who populated Main Street, the parks, beds and breakfasts, and local taverns.

However well-behaved Bella's guests were for most of the year, things turned a bit rowdy in the heat of mid-August when it came time for the annual Bella Arts and River Festival, which produced an unfortunate acronym initially overlooked by its organizers in their haste to fill a rare open weekend on the community's jam-packed schedule.

50

One enterprising local entrepreneur seized on it with imaginative T-shirts bearing the acronym, a keg, and the image of an inebriated soul and then recruited a few rock bands into the mix. It made for an invitation that spread like wildfire through the tri-state area. After awhile, as with RAGBRAI and VIESHEA, no one knew what the letters meant, except that they translated into "party time."

On the other hand, the *Bella Whig,* in deference to its older readers, had yet to use the acronym for what had become Iowa's version of spring break in Daytona Beach. Gray-haired ladies and families in minivans need not apply. Once embarrassed, Bella business people now basked in the notoriety which set the town apart from other sleepy river communities. Even occasional bad publicity, they acknowledged, is better than anonymity.

Indeed, except for that one August weekend, when Bella called upon the county sheriff's deputies for reinforcements, the city could be zoned C-F for crime-free. But the business community felt the town needed the presence of a police station and police force to reassure tourists their safety was paramount. Actually, the police station, essentially a cubicle inside City Hall, did little more than handle an occasional fender bender or report of misplaced merchandise.

"Police force" was essentially a misnomer for a

police chief and retirees who volunteered during the chief's off hours. As with many rural Iowa communities, the pay was poor, often around $10 per hour for the chief. Consequently, longevity was measured in days and weeks, rather than months and years. Few police chiefs in Bella lasted long enough to earn vacation time. Despite the image Bella tried to project, Mayberry was probably better protected when Barney Fife was in charge.

51

Tourists were blissfully unaware of the revolving door with the faux police force during the 1990s. Chiefs had been fired for failure to attend to official duties, such as responding to the rare call, including one from the mayor, or for failure to appear in court, both of which, the incumbent at the time argued, would have detracted from patrolling Main Street. They had been fired for being overly zealous in ticketing tourists, which another Bella law enforcement executive had cited as an untapped source of revenue for the department. He had earmarked a percentage for his own impoverished pocketbook, committing forgery and, by extension, tax evasion when submitting phony expense accounts.

Given those troubles, Bella city fathers and mothers were most despondent when one popular chief of three years had to be dismissed because of his failure to meet physical requirements, specifically covering 1.5 miles in 14.5 minutes on foot as part of the state agility test. Stability, city officials contended to any legislator who would listen, was more important than an obscure state mandate, noting that Bella wasn't even 1.5 miles long and few antiques aficionados or birdwatchers are perceived as having breakaway speed.

As with some other Iowa communities, Bella had become so exasperated with its investment in police chiefs—sending them to the Iowa Law Enforcement Academy only to have them depart months later— that its council publicly debated seeking reimbursement for its expenditures from those who quit or were fired. The subsequent statewide publicity made a bad situation worse, and may have scared off wannabe chiefs. Desperate to fill the position, the council hired native son, John Lawless, although he did not seem aptly named for the position.

Lawless had recently taken law enforcement courses at Hawkeye Community College, but failed to get his associate degree in criminal justice.

Still, council members were convinced a hometown boy would stay put, and that had to count for something. He was a graduate of Bella High, a former Belhawks linebacker known for his hard-hitting play. Alas, truth be told, his coaches tried to hide Lawless on defense because of his inability to ascertain opponents' most basic plays or strategy.

"John's a good kid," said Coach Rip LaFrentz, "but at some point he must have collided head on with one ballcarrier too many."

It was hardly a harbinger of detective work to come.

All things considered—a beautiful location, a town looking to make its tourism offerings year-round, and lax law enforcement—Bella was the perfect place for outside investors to target for a riverboat.

Iowa's laws governing riverboat gambling require a massive charade. For starters, riverboats are supposed to recall the days of Mark Twain and cruises with Brett Maverick-types playing card games. Yet Iowa law requires the boats to cruise only 100 days of the year, and does not regulate how many times a day or how far they must go. In fact, one riverboat was proposed for a 40-acre man-made, land-locked lake. Riverboat owners claim gamblers have an aversion to cruising and cards, preferring to come and go as they please when their arms tire from playing the slots.

Second, those holding a license must be a local non-profit group. However, that does not preclude the riverboat from being financed by another development outfit and the casino being run by a Nevada- or New Jersey-based enterprise.

It was for that reason that Lawrence Thomas and his friends from Des Moines sought out Bella innkeeper Paddy Murphy to head their group, at least in the eyes of the Iowa Racing and Gaming Commission, with the promise of a multimillion dollar harbor development.

Policing this gamesmanship—annually amounting to more than $6 billion statewide, including the lotteries—was the Iowa Division of Criminal Investigation, which, by its own admission, was strained, using one third of its personnel to probe gaming operations.

And there was John Lawless of Bella.

Two hours before the *La Bella's* maiden voyage, Pastor Paula Swenson was making some anti-riverboat gambling ripples on the airwaves during her 11 a.m. radio show on KBLA. In a sad, measured voice, she stated, "I speak to you today not as a minister of the Lord. Many of you dismiss our appeals to do what is right because you believe we are trying to impose our morals upon you. So you do not listen."

54

Then, becoming strident, she declared, "Well, this is an issue that will define your morality. It will speak to your relationship with the Lord. It is a test of your Christianity and your humanity. Gambling is a sin. Condoning gambling, which leads to the destruction of self and family, is a sin. It is not too late to take a stand and to oppose immorality. Join us today to protest this blight upon our beloved Bella."

In the 10 years since she had arrived in Bella to establish the Open Word Church of the Lord in the Woods by the River, Paula Swenson had proven to be a major irritant to community leaders and an impediment to economic development. She annually railed to no avail against the Bella Arts and River Festival, maintaining it was the second coming of Soddom and Gomorrah.

The Bella Whig called her a "misguided missionary" in an editorial. Others anxiously awaited for her to flame out and go away. Instead, she had established a foothold, largely through her radio talk show, with the time bought by parishioners' contributions. Even those who detested her, and their numbers were legion, listened to her tirades, trying to keep one step ahead of her latest campaigns.

The radio show had been the brainchild of one

Jonah Barnes, who had recognized Paula Swenson's power to persuade during her previous life, when she worked as a prostitute at the legalized brothel at Mustang Ranch in northern Nevada. Back then, the Ten Commandments were not even the Ten Suggestions for a throwaway kid who had bolted from foster homes in Fresno to make a life for herself the only way she knew how. Her only connection with the Bible had been occasional curiosity when they happened to share a motel room.

Yet she had been fascinated by the power of televangelists and mimicked them at every opportunity. When she discovered an ad in the *National Scribbler* to become a minister with the Open Word Church of the Lord for a mere $25, it was a chance to add authenticity to her act.

Enter Barnes, a Clayton County farmboy turned traveling pharmaceutical salesman, who met her during his travels to the Reno-Carson City area. He became her religious customer, figuratively and literally, seeking any excuse to return to a region he had already plied with more free samples of prescription drugs than it could handle for a decade. He was smitten and determined to remove her from a life of prostitution. He would bring her back to Iowa as Pastor Paula Swenson.

And when she had found her calling, he would betray her.

"My Jonah is my Judas," she would tell her listeners after learning he had embezzled thousands of dollars from her ministry, presumably to cash in on the harbor development.

At noon, Pastor Swenson had left the radio studio to head her protest. She was unaware of the fax that had just been transmitted to the station's newsroom from the office of Bella Police Chief John Lawless. That same fax to other news media had immediately caught the attention of *Des Moines Register* state editor Bill Watson. Without skipping a beat, he promptly called his Bella correspondent, who had just finished serving lunch and was leaving the house to cover the *La Bella's* maiden voyage.

"Charlie," he said, "what do you know about Jonah Barnes?"

"Funny you should ask," she said. "Some things had just piqued my curiosity about his involvement in the harbor development. Why? What's up?"

"According to your latest police chief, we're now dealing with the late Jonah Barnes, whose body was found on the river bank just south of the harbor," Watson said. "Get me a bio on him and any details on the embezzlement in the Courthouse files. We'll need something on his relationship with your firebrand pastor up there, too, but be careful not to indict her. I don't want her wrath—and the wrath of God—on me. We'll be sending Barry Bullyard up there to help out. We'll need something filed here no later than 5 p.m. for the state edition. You can work later for metro. This story could have legs for some time to come. Good luck."

Notebook in hand, Charlie was out the door.

Saul Shapiro was neither born nor raised in Iowa, but moved to Cedar Falls 15 years ago as editor of the Waterloo Courier *in an attempt to offset outmigration. He is a graduate of the University of California at Los Angeles with a degree in history.*

5

Very Dead

by Mary Kay Shanley

Indeed, Ken thought, the bed-and-breakfast stage production he was witnessing this particular day seemed much more fascinating than his *Wholesome American Heartland* documentary. The documentary, after all, was predictable: Let's show Middle America at work and at play. Especially at work, because that's what Middle America does best. It rises early and always eagerly, spending Monday through Friday tackling tasks with a discipline Asians would find appealing. (Still, won't the Japanese viewers be surprised to learn that most tasks in Middle America involve neither corn nor cows!) On Saturday, Middle America cleans houses and tends yards. And on Sunday, it rests. (Well, maybe not the Rev. Paula Swenson.)

Somewhere in between all of this work, Middle America plays. Board games, Ken had supposed— just like in Jane Smiley's *A Thousand Acres*—although he had to admit that during his several months of crisscrossing the Heartland, he hadn't seen a single family wrap an evening around Monopoly.

Even before today, the thought had begun to gnaw at Ken that he might be approaching this assignment with preconceived notions—not a good thing for a good journalist to do. And he was a good journalist. Nobody at breakfast disputed that, although discussion of his professional ability provided the basis for some pretty interesting dialogue.

"If I'd said Ken was a good journalist, you would have wanted proof!" Charlie had snapped at Spence. There was a clear implication that if Spence had said such a thing, it would have been a statement of fact which required no proof. Then she'd smacked her wet dish cloth (she called it a rag) on the cutting board. And there was trembling and a quivering voice and at the peak of the crescendo, she'd said very loudly and clearly, "OUT!" to Spence, pointing toward the door (as though directions were necessary).

All of which Ken dutifully wrote down within 30 minutes precisely because he was a good journalist. (But not a mind reader, although that wasn't information he chose to share with the others in the kitchen. Let them think what they may.)

If that incident had been all there was to the bed-and-breakfast production, Ken might have spent more internal time wrestling with the possibility that he had subconsciously put together the *Wholesome American Heartland* documentary while he was still on the plane. Then, all one must do after leaving O'Hare in a rented car is to shoot footage that reflects the preconceived story. Such an approach had not been his intention. But journalists—especially those who've been reporting for years—run the risk of producing what they assume is the truth, rather than actually looking for it. Laziness, one may call it. Or complacency. It's to be guarded against.

So it was that Spence's unexpected return to Three Sisters later that morning piqued Ken's professional senses—reminding him that stories lay in wait everywhere. And that such stories are almost always more interesting than the predictability a journalist must guard against.

It occurred to Ken the minute he spotted Spence's Lexus coming down the street that Charlie hadn't been gone much more than a minute or two—to the library, she'd announced. Spence pulled slowly up to the curb across from Three Sisters and parked. When he didn't get out, Ken decided to walk over to him. The driver's window was cracked open and Spence was still behind the wheel, deep in thought. He seemed startled when Ken leaned down close to the window and asked if he were okay.

"Yeah. Just needed to get something out of the house," Spence had said. He didn't seem interested in elaborating, so Ken brought up the only subject the two men had in common: Charlie. Very quickly Ken realized that this discussion—through a crack in the window, no less—was going nowhere either, and he stepped back so Spence could get out of the car. As Spence strode past him, across the street and up the front walk, Ken turned and headed south, toward the corner. He rounded it and, on an impulse he didn't yet clearly understand, doubled back to the gravel parking lot behind Three Sisters where his Hertz Probe was parked.

The Probe was nondescript—all white, which Kiyoko, his ex-wife, always hated. "White cars look like they belong to salesmen," she would say. Then, she'd shudder a little, as though nothing could be worse than to make your living selling something. Once Ken considered pointing out to her that he sold words and images for a living, but decided against it.

The Probe was registered in Illinois, but because Bella was a stone's throw from that state, the license plate wouldn't attract attention. Maybe, Ken thought, it might be interesting to see where Spence was going today. Or whom he was visiting. (And what was it he had to get from the house, anyway?)

Following Spence around, Ken thought, could be far more interesting than shooting footage of Middle America. Then he remembered—he'd committed to video-taping Pastor Paula down at the dock. But the morning was still young—with time for sleuthing as well as filming.

Jonah Barnes was very dead. Even John Lawless, who had failed to receive his associate degree in criminal justice after taking law enforcement courses at Hawkeye Community College, could tell that. At first, of course, the police chief didn't realize it was Jonah Barnes's body that he saw on the river bank just south of the harbor. But he certainly knew it was a dead one. That was clear to Chief Lawless even as he sat behind the wheel of his squad car (actually, Bella's only squad car) up on the road.

He'd been in his city hall cubicle—which his wife, Lori Lawless, referred to as his "command post"— for most of the morning. Resting up, as it were, for the big afternoon.

"Everybody'll be here for the *La Bella* maiden voyage," he'd told Lori at breakfast. "Lawyer-types and DCI guys and the media. It's gonna be lots more than just tourists today. I'll probably have to say a few words at the ceremony." He paused to stir a heaping teaspoon of sugar into his black coffee.

"It'll be kind of reassuring I bet to hear from me. You know, tell folks that law and order is alive and well in Bella."

That's when Lori suggested Chief Lawless might want to go down to the command post and pull some of his thoughts together. Which is exactly what he was doing when his office phone rang. It was Old Jim Hulbert (similar to Poor Ellen Gutcheon), calling to say he'd been walking down by the harbor, looking for a quiet place to fish when he saw this guy "a-lyin on the sand, Chief, and he looked mighty dead to me. So I just didn't go nowhere's near him cuz I can't be getting mixed up in somethin' like this. I'm on Social Security."

Thus it was that Chief Lawless never did get to finish planning his remarks for the maiden voyage of the *La Bella Riverboat*. Not that it mattered because Chief Lawless wasn't listed on the program to begin with, but now he had much bigger stuff to worry about.

So here he was, looking down the embankment at this dead body in the sand. He took a deep breath, got out of his squad car and shut the door. He patted the holster that rode his left hip and ran his hand over the club on his right hip before starting down the fairly steep slope that separated the county road from the beach.

Jonah lay face up in the sand. He'd been shot at close range in the chest and since there was no gun around, the Chief immediately ruled out suicide. Jonah's white shirt was frayed where the bullet had entered, and there was a powder burn around the hole. His face was distorted, his eyes opened wide. The Chief noted with some curiosity that Jonah looked surprised (if, indeed, a dead person can do that). The blood in his mouth and ears was still fresh. Chief Lawless couldn't tell if rigor mortis had begun to set in without touching the body. And if he remembered anything, it was that he should not be touching that body.

Next, the Chief looked around the area of the body. The sand was fairly even—not messed up as though there'd been a struggle. Certainly Jonah had not been dragged to the site. In fact, by the footprints, it appeared that Jonah had walked down the beach from one direction and somebody else had walked from the other, probably surprised Jonah with a gun, shot him and walked back the same way he'd come from. Or she'd come from. The Chief couldn't say whether the footprints belonged to a man or woman.

Since he hadn't worked many murder cases—actually, none—Chief Lawless figured he'd done good to get this far with his deductive reasoning skills.

"I guess I better be callin' Gene," he said out loud to no one at all. He turned and retraced his own footprints to the embankment, climbed up and reached in the car to grab his police radio. "I'm callin' for Sheriff Gene Schmidt," he announced. "This here's John Lawless and I'm reportin' a murder."

The significance of that statement was not lost on Chief John Lawless, who realized that he could serve in Bella, Iowa, until he was 100 and probably never again utter those words.

Intellectually, Jonah Barnes was somewhere between John Lawless and Spence Wood. He wasn't as street smart as Dixie Clark—but then, it took her four husbands to get street smart. He wasn't as flamboyant as Paddy Murphy nor as nice as Lawrence Thomas, the La Bella Corporation fellow who kept putting business aside to watch birds. He didn't have Charlie Andropolous's drive, nor Ken Wakabayashi's curiosity. But he sure had an interesting past.

And Pastor Paula Swenson was only a part of that past.

Jonah grew up on the family farm—a century farm at that —along with twin sisters a year younger than he. Of the 350 acres his father owned, 290 were tillable. When Jonah was a kid, the family also raised cattle and hogs. But as the face of farming began to change, it became clear to Earl Barnes that small livestock operations would soon be a thing of the past. By the time Jonah was graduated from Bella High, Earl was crop farming only, with profits so slim that either more land or a second income was a necessity. So he added another 100 acres on a cash rent basis and his wife, Edna, took a clerical assistant position at the First State Bank in Bella. Jonah the Graduate farmed, pumped gas, and secretly harbored a desire to be a nurse. A year later, his sisters graduated and enrolled at Iowa State, one in engineering, the other in accounting. When Earl announced that "those jobs sounded like something a man would be doing," Jonah knew that his becoming a nurse was out of the question.

So at age 20, he enrolled in a biology class at Peosta Community College as well as in a you-can-sell-anything correspondence course he saw advertised in *Iowa Singles*. Within two years he'd taken every life science offering on the community college campus, plus he had a Certificate of Completion AND a Diploma of Accomplishment from the sales course people. Most importantly, though, Jonah actually believed that he could sell anything. His first job was with Alliance Pharmaceuticals, a start-up company based in Kansas City. He traveled Iowa, Nebraska, Minnesota, and the Dakotas, introducing doctors to Mertriptan, a new product for migraine sufferers. Jonah's down-home approach, his core knowledge (and, yes, probably love) of life sciences and the natural high he got from being on the road worked in his favor. Within 18 months, Jonah was Alliance's top sales rep.

Nobody was more surprised about that than Jonah unless, of course, it was his father who periodically suggested Jonah settle down back home and invest his profits in farmland. After all, Earl noted on more than one occasion, 390 tillable acres wouldn't be enough to sustain a family down the road.

"And besides," he'd always add, "that's a lot of acres for somebody who is getting along in years to be farming by himself."

But instead of going back home to Bella, Jonah

went to Reno. He won the first trip there through Alliance and had so much fun he kept going back on his own dime. To keep the family from worrying, he told them that Alliance was expanding, mainly in the southwest. (It was in their long-range plans.) Earl didn't like the trips to Nevada since they didn't fit in anywhere with his long-range vision for the Barnes Family Farms operation. And the twins never did buy Jonah's reason for the trips. But they were mum about it whenever the family gathered back home around the dinner table.

So it was that for a couple of years Jonah Barnes would load one suitcase with clothes and the other with Mertriptan to distribute on behalf of the company and head off for Nevada every chance he got. But since he only went to Reno and Carson City, and since he couldn't officially call on the doctors there, his distribution was limited to employees at the Mustang Ranch, a couple of desk clerks in Carson City, some bartenders, and anybody who happened to be on the next barstool late of evenings.

One night, the person on the next barstool turned out to be another Iowan—a guy from Des Moines who was fresh out of law school at the University of Iowa. He'd heard of tourist towns like Bella and Galesburg, Illinois, but had not visited there. Still, when he was a kid, he saw the Bílý Brothers Clocks in Spillville, took a boat ride through Spook Cave, and watched the locks on the Mississippi open and close as barges went through. "That was one of our family vacations," the lawyer said. "I'll never forget the locks. They were fascinating. Just fascinating."

Jonah always had been fascinated by the locks as well. So with that experience as common ground, the two men bought each other a second—or maybe it was a third—beer. Before the evening was over, they discovered, much to their own surprise, that they had another experience in common. A young woman named Paula at the Mustang Ranch.

Mary Kay Shanley grew up in Webster City, Iowa. After graduating from Creighton University in Omaha, she became a reporter for The Des Moines Register. *She has been a free-lance writer for* The Register *and national magazines since 1969. Her first book,* She Taught Me to Eat Artichokes, *was released in 1993. Since then, she has had four other books published.*

Mary Kay has taught at Iowa State and Drake and teaches in the University of Iowa Summer Writing Festival. She and her husband, Dennis Rhodes, live in West Des Moines. They have a daughter in San Francisco, a daughter in Boston and a son in Princeton. She also has two Shelties who sleep under her desk all day long.

6

Pastor in the Fog

by Jean Florman

"Jesus Christ!"

As Charlie pitched forward, she hit her head on a sweet gum tree that clung to the embankment behind Three Sisters. She teetered, then flailed until she caught the arm of the figure she had ploughed into as she half-slid, half-fell down the bluff toward the crime scene.

The figure hollered, "Let go!" and Charlie jumped like a squirrel on a high-tension wire. Then everything snapped into focus.

Pastor Paula looked dumfounded—dumfounded and dirty. In the enveloping early afternoon fog, her wide dark eyes and thin face reminded Charlie of a startled ferret. Later, Charlie would realize she had been as stunned by the pastor's profanity as she was by her presence here in the scrub along the Mississippi.

"Pastor Paula! What are you doing here?"

"What *am* I doing here? What *am* I doing here?" The pastor's voice trailed off into a forlorn wail. She rubbed the side of her wet face with one hand, leaving pale finger-painted stripes of mud on her cheek. Then she breathed deeply, looked pointedly at Charlie, and demanded, "What am *I* doing here?"

Pastor Paula turned and stumbled past Charlie, walking unevenly along the embankment toward town until she disappeared into the gathering mist.

Charlie had the feeling she had missed something. She shook her head quickly to regain her senses and continued down the soggy undergrowth toward the river.

70

By the time she got there, there was nothing much to see and everybody in the county was there to see it. In a small town, news about birth, death, and sex travels telepathically. And a murder—well, everybody not only knew what, they knew who, why, and when Oprah was coming.

Charlie could hear it now. By tomorrow morning, Dixie would be serving up reports of the latest convoluted theory as fast as Charlie could coax the cheese blintzes off the griddle.

"Leona Griswold finally came in for a perm yesterday," Dixie would offer, pondering which cinnamon sugar donut hole to tackle next and watching Charlie swirl blintz batter as the guests waited patiently at the table.

"She says it was a new Mafia family in Chicago. The Primo Dons, or something like that. They've wormed their way into town through the pizza concession on the *La Bella*. Hell, if they'd send Pacino down, I'd join right up myself. You know, Leona really needs a wax."

As Charlie rubbed her sore head and jogged toward the crime scene crowd, she smiled. Dixie had her faults, but under that nail-spitting exterior, she really was an angel.

In the dank early afternoon air, the crowd had become a living thing, the organic fusion of all its parts. No single voice rose above the others—just a low buzz of humanity. As Charlie reached the edge of the crowd, it parted as though on cue to let the body through. A minute later a car door thunked and the hearse glided off through the gloom.

"Stand back! Stand back!" From beyond the yellow police ribbon, Chief Lawless flapped like a rooster guarding his harem. "OK, ladies and gentlemen, time to go home! No need to hang around anymore. Please, leave the investigating to the experts."

"Yeah, Chief," Charlie thought, "you think that's you." She approached the police cordon.

"The show's over, miss. Nothing more to see. Nothing. No more. Nope. Nada." Chief Lawless darted around like a spindly-legged shore bird hopping from one spot to another in search of unseen treasures buried in the sand. We all live on hope, Charlie thought.

"It's me, Chief Lawless. Charlie Andropolous. Remember? I own the Three Sisters Inn. But actually, that's not why I'm here. I'm here to do a story for the *Des Moines Register*."

Lawless sliced a cone of light through the fog with his flashlight, and Charlie stepped into it. In the background, she could see a slow *pas de tois* of other officers searching the ground, bending down, standing, searching, bending, standing, searching. Outside help, Charlie thought.

"Oh, Charlie, yes, of course," Lawless stood up straighter and tipped up his hat to smooth his thinning hair. "How can I help you?"

"Gosh, I know you don't want to answer questions right now," Charlie lied, "but I wanted to make sure the facts got out before all the rumors ran too far amuck."

"Well, that's a good point," Chief Lawless said more loudly than necessary, "but you know, we don't have much yet. I can tell you, however, that the deceased has been tentatively identified as Jonah Barnes, and that he was shot at close range in the chest."

Gee thanks, Charlie thought, that's as much as I got from Bill Watson. But then the chief spoke again, apparently warming to the task.

"We know, for instance, that one of those environmentalist birdwatchers was back here yesterday," Lawless said, "and he claims he didn't see anything unusual. He did find a dead beaver, however. You know those protestors were lucky to find a dead beaver to burn in effigy because all those pro-ecology people are pro-animal rights too and they wouldn't have wanted to kill one just to burn it. And then this one just turned up with its head bashed in. Road kill."

Charlie was having a hard time following the drift of the story, let alone getting it on paper. Then the chief added, "You know, your place is the closest one up the bluff from here, so we'll want to talk with you and your guests," he hooked his thumbs in his wide leather gun belt, "just to see if anybody noticed anything out of the ordinary."

Charlie decided to beg.

"Come on, John, is there anything else, anything at all I can take to my editor to show him I've been busting my butt here? I've got a deadline coming up."

Chief Lawless leaned forward and lowered his voice. "Well, a while ago, I did spot something interesting. Burn evidence."

"Well," Charlie said holding her breath against the ripe smell of chewing tobacco, "you know high school kids sometimes have fires down here on the beach. Maybe it was just left over trash."

"Don't think so, no ma'am, no. No signs of a bonfire. Just burned paper—right next to the body."

Hook, line, and sinker. But as one of the state crime lab investigators approached, Chief Lawless suddenly drew himself tall and adopted an official tone. "I'll contact you as soon as anything comes up, Ms. Andropolous. Thanks for your advice. We'll be sure to check it out."

I didn't give you any advice, Charlie grumbled as she trudged back up the embankment toward town, and you didn't give me much of a lead. As she reached the top of the bluff, Charlie noticed a lurid pink glow. The fog was casting the light from the riverboat casino back across the town. Charlie looked at the *La Bella*, where a sign in flamingo-pink neon flashed the images of a clock and a pair of dice. Time to take a chance.

As she walked down Main Street toward Bella, to see if the maiden voyage would be delayed by the fog, Charlie ran into Dixie tottering out of Joe's Bar and Grille. More the former than the latter, Joe's had been a fixture in town since long before the gambling interests had moved in. Dixie had something of a crush on Joe himself, although she swore that he was born lazy and then had a setback. At the moment, she seemed to have had a few too many after-lunch daiquiris.

"Hi, Charlie!" she sang out. "Dixie's tipsy." Only it came out, Dipsy's tixy. Both women laughed. The mascara on Dixie's left eye was smeared.

"Come on, Gorgeous," Charlie said. "You need to sober up. And you have to help me with dinner so I can work on this story."

The two women turned the corner at Schweigart's Funeral Home. Like most Midwestern small-town mortuaries, it was the only game in town. Three generations of morticians ago, it had been converted from a white clapboard turn-of-the-century four-square, the kind families used to order complete from Sears & Roebuck, nails and all. Now the hearse carrying Jonah Barne's body was parked beneath the porte couchere, which had been added on to protect both the living and the dead from the elements. On the front porch a sign said, "Schweigart's Funeral Home. We Go The Distance For You."

"How the hell far could that be?" Dixie asked as they walked past.

Charlie laughed, and Dixie added, "Vera Purifoy came in for a tint last week and filled me in on the latest on Jonah Barnes' folks. Can you believe that woman forced her ailing Swedish mother to become a U.S. citizen so she can inherit more? And the old man made their twin daughters pay for their own braces."

"Sounds like they were meant for each other."

The two women crossed the street in front of the Feather Anchor, a literary oasis that specialized in children's picture books, handmade jewelry, and blank books waiting for writers to reveal their secrets.

"You wait," Dixie said, "Some day, I'm going write something that'll hit the top of the best-seller list like a water skipper riding Old Faithful. Next thing you know, I'll be doing readings at the Feather Anchor."

"Right, Dix, but first you have to sleep this one off. Not to change the subject or anything, but the weirdest thing just happened."

"Yeah, I know," Dixie said. "Something exciting happened in Bella, Iowa. That's pretty weird, all right. God, my head feels like an overripe muskmelon on steroids."

She sank onto a park bench.

"Come on," Charlie tugged her friend back to her feet. "You need to get home. And I've got a story to start working on. Plus zucchini bread. But listen up. I was running down the bluff to check out the Barnes scene, and I ran right into Pastor Paula. She looked scared—scared and dirty. I couldn't tell if she'd been down there with everyone else gawking at the spectacle, but she sure wasn't taking the easy way back to town. And her face was either very sweaty or very teary."

"Volume two!" Dixie shouted and punched her fist toward the sky. "That woman really frosts me. She's gonna be volume two of my series about all the crazies in this town." She shot a wicked look at Charlie and added, "I'm starting with you."

Jean Florman's work has appeared in various publications, including The Washington Post, Minnesota Monthly, The Iowan, Iowa Woman, *and Meredith Corporation's* Country Home. *For five years she has been a commentator and producer for KUNI, and her book* Moments in Iowa History *was based on her 1996 daily series for the public radio station. Jean's 1998 weekly series,* Moldboard to Motherboard *explored the role of technology in 20th-century Iowa. She has taught writing for the University of Iowa Summer Writing Festival and the National Wildlife Federation.*

She's learned a lot about writing from her children, Amber and Brian, as well as from The University of Iowa MFA Program in Nonfiction Writing. For years Jean has wanted to write fiction just so she could introduce a character named Purifoy.

7

If You Build It, They Will Come

by Robert F. Baldwin

"Bella, Bella, Bella," wailed Charlie, as she walked briskly through the foggy, cobbled streets of the picturesque river town.

Dixie wove, but didn't quite stagger, and managed to keep up. They merged with the growing throng of pedestrians who streamed toward the lights of the gaudy, gleaming Gommorah that floated and glowed in the harbor like a fogbound neon palace.

"This town is beginning to test my journalistic resolve," Charlie mumbled. "What a day!"

The city's first floating casino ready to cast off for her maiden voyage, a visit from a major TV celebrity, a very dead body, and the afternoon was still young. In addition, her editor wanted her to run down a bio of the dead person—a mysterious deacon who may also have been an embezzler.

But not even her editor knew that the deceased might also have paved the way for the floating casino his pastor vehemently opposed. Was his death related in some way to the grand opening of the *La Bella*?

"April Fool," Charlie said to Dixie "This town's

plumb full of April Fools, dead and alive, and I guess I'm one of them."

She'd felt a surge of resentment when Bill Watson had told her he was sending Barry Bullyard to Bella to give her a hand, as if she couldn't handle things herself. She had wanted to scream at him, "I don't *need* help."

Nevertheless, she acknowledged, it was getting harder and harder to know when to write, when to research, and when to bake zucchini bread for her guests.

"But so what," she told Dixie. "I'll show them." This whole thing, she was beginning to sense, went a lot deeper than anyone suspected and she was going to get to the bottom of it.

She was glad she had laid down the law to Spence that morning and confident that Mister Know-it-All was finally out of her life. He had been right about one thing, though — it didn't look right for a journalist to be reporting on events in which her ex-husband was involved as an attorney. But it wasn't a conflict of interest. No way. No matter how much dirt she might uncover, she wasn't going to flinch if any of it fell on Mr. Spence Wood.

"I *am* a good journalist," she said aloud, remembering Ken's words at the table that morning.

"I never shed you weren't," her inebriated friend grinned.

"Let's not start *that* again," said Charlie.

As they drew near the harbor, the women could hear and see a female vocalist in an evening dress covered with dazzling red sequins, singing a jazzy version of "There'll Be a Hot Time in the Old Town Tonight," accompanied by a 12-piece banjo orchestra, flown in from San Diego. The singer and musicians stood together on the deck of the ship and all wore matching flat-top straw boaters. The banjoists wore red and white seersucker blazers, navy blue trousers, and white shoes

Near the wharf, a huge crowd watched as Oprah Winfrey's TV crew pointed cameras first at the musicians, then at a growing pile of gambling paraphernalia and dead animals around which a group of placard-toting environmental activists and members of the Open Word Church of the Lord in the Woods by the River were allowing themselves to be interviewed.

Oprah was questioning an elder of the church as the two women arrived. ". . . a bonfire of protest, right here by the wharf?"

"That's right, just as soon as the devil's playground over yonder gets under way, but we're not sure when that will be, because of the fog," said the interviewee, a portly man in a sport coat. As he spoke, one of the camera people zoomed in on a button he was wearing: "Sin Floats."

"Who's going to be lighting the fire?" Oprah asked.

"Our pastor."

"And which one of you is the pastor?"

"She's not here yet. She's late, but the ship can't leave before the fog clears a bit, so we're not worried."

"If she doesn't get here in time, one of us will

light it," shouted a man carrying a placard with a drawing of a beaver gazing sadly at a riverboat with tears rolling down its furry cheeks. Below the picture, a caption proclaimed: "The Odds Are Against Us." The camera crew turned their lenses in the direction of the placard.

"No, no," the man with the button was saying. "It's a symbolic fire and it must be lit by one of the brethren."

"Aren't all of you members of the same church?" Oprah asked.

"Only half of us," said the man with the "Sin Floats" button. "But we welcome the involvement of anyone who opposes the sin of gambling, even if it's just secular humanists who are trying to save the lives of a few poor, worthless but otherwise innocent creatures."

"How about that, you environmentalists. Do any of you agree that fish and beavers are 'worthless creatures'?"

"Let's hear it for beaver!" shouted a young bystander in a B.A.R.F. sweatshirt.

"I'd like to stay and watch this, but I've got to do some interviews of my own," Charlie said. As she and Dixie approached the gangplank, the singer in the red dress launched into a new song. A uniformed casino employee wearing a paisley vest and a black garter around the sleeve of his white shirt was collecting tickets. Another young man in a pale green B.A.R.F. shirt was trying, unsuccessfully, to talk his way aboard.

Charlie noticed that her friend's face was the same

color as the young man's shirt. "You better jus' go 'long w'out me," Dixie said and disappeared among the throngs milling about on the wharf.

In the main salon, Charlie watched as invited guests, officials, and tourists who had managed to book passage on the cruise, milled about, chatting.

The craps, blackjack, roulette, and other gaming tables were ready but idle, and strips of red, white and blue plastic ribbon had been hung as boundaries to keep gamblers away from the slot machines until the moment the floating casino would cast off and the gaming would officially begin.

Surely, Charlie thought, there must be people aboard—members of the La Bella Corporation, in particular—who could tell her things about Deacon Barnes and his connection to the casino, but at the moment she saw no one she recognized except Doris and Mary Lou who were waiting expectantly near the idle slot machines, their faces glowing with anticipatory pleasure. She wondered if any other guests from the Three Sisters would show up.

"So far, I am a lonely bus token," said a familiar voice just behind her. Charlie turned and found herself face to face with the nice mind reader from Japan whose first name was still a mystery.

"Why hello, Elvis," she quipped. "I'm afraid I don't understand."

"Token Asian. But that will change, believe me. If you build it, we will come." He drew close and whispered in her ear, "It is a well-known fact that we Asians can't resist gambling. Especially in America. Especially when we have seen it on film or video."

He patted the camera he was carrying.

He was probably right. She remembered the day last year when she'd been in Des Moines and had driven out to Winterset because she felt obliged to make at least one trip to the Eastwood-Streep memorial covered bridge. While she had been there, two buses drove up, parked, and disgorged about 100 female Japanese tourists who spent an hour taking pictures of each other and tacking love letters to the wooden timbers inside the bridge. After they'd left, she'd tried to read a few of them, but she couldn't find any that were in English.

"Like *The Bridges of Madison County*," Ken continued.

"Ken, sometimes I could swear you can read my mind."

"Oh, really?" he replied with an enigmatic smile. You were thinking about that love story? Very popular in my country."

"So I've noticed."

"Did you ever leave a note at the bridge?" Ken asked.

"For whom? It would have been a futile gesture on the part of a lonely, bus token gringo."

"Some people," said Ken, "believe there are no boundaries to the love between men and women. That's what I told your husband this morning after you left."

"Ex-husband. Almost."

"Ex or not, I found him quite interesting and, I might add, he was having an interesting morning. If there are boundaries, he will find them."

At that moment, a portion of the salon became brightly illuminated by the lights of Oprah's camera crew. Basking giddily in the light were Doris and Mary Lou, whose matching Queen of Hearts shirts had caught the eye of America's most popular TV talk show hostess.

"I gather by your shirts that both of you are poker players?" Oprah was saying.

"Not really," said Doris. "We prefer crapshooting."

"*Used* to prefer crapshooting," Mary Lou interjected. "Frankly, the name always seemed a bit crude to me. Now we prefer roulette. Who could resist the elegance of 'le rouge and le noir?"

Through one of the windows of the salon, Charlie spied her nice boarder from the La Bella Corporation, Lawrence Thomas, standing outside, alone on the deck. He was wearing the strap of his binoculars around his neck and he appeared to be scanning the shore of the harbor, perhaps looking for wildlife that had survived the developers.

Charlie turned to Ken and said, "Excuse me, whatever your real first name is, but I'm working on an assignment and just spotted someone I ought to interview. "

"No problem," said Ken. "We can talk later about the strange comings and goings of Mr. Wood."

As Charlie joined Lawrence Thomas near the after rail of the ship she could see a few blue patches of sky overhead. "Did you enjoy your early birding expedition this morning?" she asked.

Thomas lowered the binoculars and studied Charlie for a moment before replying. "Oh, yes, thor-

oughly. And I so much enjoyed the tea and croissants you left for me. I'm sorry I didn't have time to
meet with you this morning. Things have been so
hectic."

"You don't look very hectic right now," Charlie
said, smiling.

"Ah, my dear lady, appearances can deceive. But
actually, you are quite right. Now that the ship is
ready to sail, my day's work is almost over." He raised
the glasses to his eyes and began studying the shoreline again.

"That's good," said Charlie, "because there's
something I need to ask you."

"About my accommodations?" he asked, still looking through the glasses.

"No, no, not at all. I wanted to find out how well
you knew Jonah Barnes."

He lowered the binoculars and looked at her carefully. She was aware that from inside the main salon
Ken was pointing his camera through the window at
her and Thomas.

"Barnes?" said Thomas. "Never heard of him. Who
is Jonah Barnes?"

"You mean 'Who was Jonah Barnes?' Or haven't
you heard?"

"Heard what?"

"The body of Deacon Jonah Barnes of Pastor
Swenson's church was found down by the shore this
morning, not far from the Three Sisters."

"My God! No, I hadn't heard a thing. And you
mean to tell me that this man, this Deacon Barnes,
was involved, religiously, that is, with the same

woman who's been threatening to take the La Bella Corporation to court?"

"Well, yes, but I assumed you knew that."

He studied her carefully. "What makes you think I would know anything about this. . . this Mr. Barnes?"

"Well some years ago I'd heard him mentioned in connection with the development of the harbor, and I just assumed that the La Bella Corporation . . ."

Her words were drowned out by a blast from the boat's whistle, followed by a voice that could be heard throughout the ship and on the wharf.

"Ladies and Gentlemen, this is your captain, Myron Tucker, speaking to you from the *La Bella* wheelhouse. The fog has begun to burn off and I have given orders to the crew to prepare to cast off."

When the captain finished his announcement, Thomas spoke to her again. "Sorry, my dear lady, but I'm afraid I can't recall anyone named Barnes in connection with the harbor project. And now, you'll have to excuse me. Duty beckons." As he departed, he added, "I'll ask Mr. Murphy if he knows anything about this Barnes fellow."

Charlie started to follow him, but thought better of it. Just then a commotion near the wharf caught her attention and she noticed a curl of smoke rising from the pile of gambling equipment, dead fish, and beaver. A few licks of orange flame had begun to appear. As the flames climbed higher, the church members and environmentalists took a few steps backward, away from the heat. Charlie noted that Pastor Paula was not among them.

The crew let go the mooring lines and tossed them to the dock. The powerful diesel engines throbbed and the make-believe paddle wheel of the Disneyfied riverboat began to turn. The banjo orchestra played and the vocalist sang.

Big wheel keep on turnin'
Proud Mary keep on burnin'
Rollin' Rollin''. . .

As the ship moved out into the river, the captain's voice again echoed through the ship, introducing "your friend and neighbor, gracious innkeeper, and president of the enterprise that will lead Bella into a prosperous new millennium . . . Paddy Murphy!"

Paddy, in turn, spoke on behalf of the corporation. "Ladies and gentleman, fellah-Bellans, gracious guests, and patrons of riverboat gaming," he intoned. "I am proud to welcome you aboard Iowa's newest, most palatial, sophisticated and elegant floating casino. I'm not going to bore you with any long-winded speeches. I will simply say that from this moment forward, Bella is where the action is so let the action begin!"

A deafening cheer filled the main salon of the *La Bella*. Amid the cheers, and a few whistles, in walked Tricia LeBlanc, the Delaware County Pork Queen from down river, and Misty Russell, the reigning Miss La Bella of 1998. The two young ladies carried a huge pair of scissors with which they snipped through the red, white and blue ribbon that had separated the suckers from the slots. Within moments, coins were dropping into the the machines like golden kernels of Pioneer hybrid falling into a grain hopper at harvest time. The sound of whirling machinery, jackpot bells, and dice clacking as they cascaded across green felt tables blended into a resonant and hypnotic tone.

Doris and Mary Lou, eagerly feeding quarters into three slot machines apiece, agreed that they'd try roulette before the day was out, but not until their arms got tired.

On shore, the bonfire was roaring high. As the ship pulled out into the current of the Mississippi, the man with the "Sin Floats" button cupped his hands and shouted after it, "This fire ain't near as hot as where that ship is going to carry all of you!"

But no one aboard the *La Bella* was listening.

Robert F. Baldwin is the author of This is the Sea that Feeds Us *and other books for children*
His web address is:
http://www.geocities.com/Paris/1659/

8

The Sinner and the Sin

by Mary Swander

"Everybody back," John Lawless said, trying to keep the crushing crowd away from the corpse that had washed up on shore. "Back," he commanded, holding up his hand. Still, the throng pressed in around him.

Just a hundred yards from the Three Sisters, the body of a man in a charcoal suit lay on the rocks, waterlogged, his hair plastered down to his scalp. His white shirt had taken on the muddy grey color of the Mighty Mississippi River. His face was as white as the string of loose clouds that floated through the sky. A sole eagle, the last to leave for the spring, perched on the dark branches of an oak tree. It spread its long wings and glided out over the water, then in over the dead man, then back to the tree, staring straight ahead, surveying. The dead man stared face down into the rocky shore, his hands splayed out at his sides. A single brick was tied to his foot. A dead beaver lay next to him.

John Lawless stepped over to his squad car. "Gene," he whispered into the phone to the sheriff. "I'm going to need some help down here at the dock. Quick. Roger."

"Could we take that shot again, Chief?" one of the national news photographers called. "We'd like to get a good picture of you by your squad car, you know, local cop with the dead guy in the background, the mist and fog burning off the river. What's the name of this river, anyway? We'll need that for the caption. We're going for a cover story here on the *New York Times Magazine*."

"The which?" John Lawless said, his eyes blinking into the flashing lights.

"Who is this guy, Chief?" another reporter shouted. "Give us a name."

"Why, isn't that the handsome fellow who ate breakfast with us?" Doris asked Mary Lou. The two gambling fanatics, who had just returned from *La Bella's* maiden voyage, turned to each other, their jaws hanging open.

"My stars, I believe it is. I could swear on a stack of Bibles that I sat right next to him eating my frittata."

John Lawless knew he was going to eat his $10/hour salary if he didn't get the crowd away from the body. A band of Bella teenagers in nose rings, black boots and B.A.R.F. T-shirts orbited around the corpse. The photographers were crawling over the rocks, taking shots from every angle. Oprah Winfrey stood on the second story deck of the *La Bella*, microphone in hand, describing the entire scene. Ken, the Japanese man who had been hanging around town, was videotaping the whole event from the edge of the crowd. And even Lawrence Thomas was peering down from the deck through a pair of birding binoculars.

"A name, Chief," the reporters hounded.

But neither John Lawless nor the Bella towns-people needed to be given a name. They knew Spence Wood as well as they knew their Uncle George. Who else would come to town driving a shiny foreign car like that? Each time Poor Ellen Gutcheon had her hair done, she filled in the girls at her coffee klatch. Yes, he and Charlie are getting divorced, but he still comes to visit sometimes. Goodness. Spends the night, too. I've seen him coming down the walk in the morning just as I arrive for my appointment. No, no, that fancy car had been there all night. Can you beat that? I'd think that once I'd separated from my husband, I wouldn't want to go and shack up with him again. Oh, yes, I've heard that too. He pays the mortgage. I guess she pays in the end, too. Gracious.

"Now get away," John Lawless shouted.

Margaret, the Boston terrier bulldog, sniffed at the pantleg of the corpse and Paddy Murphy's mutt licked its face.

"Git, git, git," John Lawless threw a rock at the dogs. If this circus kept up, all the forensic evidence was going to be damaged. Gone. Gone forever. First one dead body, then another. What was Bella coming to? What was happening? You open the state to gambling, and then before you know it, you've got innocent people dropping down dead at your feet. What a pile up. This was worse than the football games that Bella used to lose to Dubuque Wahlert.

Speaking of feet, John Lawless thought, Spence has that brick tied around his foot. Now that is real curious. Who could rule on that? Murder or suicide?

"Step aside, people, step aside," Henry Maguire said. As county coroner, he was trying to make his way through the crowd to pronounce Spence officially dead. Dixie trotted along at Henry's elbow, carrying his bag with the death certificate forms.

"That's Spence, all right," Dixie said. "Dead as a doornail. I'll just fill in his name on this certificate, Doc. Then you can sign it."

Dixie glanced up at Henry, her eyelashes flickering. "I could've told you Spence would come to a no good end. In his own way, he was way worse than any of the Dicks I ever had. Delbert, Dwayne, Darryl, and Dewey. At least with them, it was over when it was over. . . . Oh, my God!" Dixie shrieked.

"What is it?" Henry asked. He crouched down next to the corpse, his ear next to Spence's mouth, just to make certain he was no longer breathing.

"That brick!" Dixie took a few steps back, the pen falling out of her hand.

Margaret pawed at the rope that held the brick to Spence's foot. "Grrr-rough," she growled. Paddy Murphy's mutt took a dump at the base of the *New York Times* reporter's tripod.

"That brick belongs to the Three Sisters Inn," Dixie said. "We use it to hold the door shut."

"Do you now?" John Lawless asked. He reached back into his squad car, again contacting the sheriff. "Gene, we got us a clue here. Exhibition #1. Roger."

"I'm on my way," Gene said. "Roger."

The metallic wail of Gene Schmidt's squad car siren merged with Charlie's human wail when she arrived at the river bank. She and Mrs. Pillsly pushed and shoved their way through the crowd until they were standing over Spence. Professionally, Charlie knew that she should join the other reporters and try to glean all the facts about this death, but personally, she just couldn't. Instead, she collapsed into a ball on the ground, crying and shaking. Mrs. Pillsly stood rigidly by, a strand of hair falling out of her bun.

"There, there," a voice said, and then Charlie felt a hand on her shoulder.

Charlie glanced up into Ken's deep eyes. "I'm afraid I can't be a good journalist today," she cried.

"Well, not at this very moment anyway," Ken said, helping her to her feet.

"I know I'm not supposed to care," Charlie said.

"It's normal. He'd been your husband."

"It's the ex-wife!" the journalists shouted almost in a chorus, rushing toward Charlie.

"Was he suicidal?" one asked.

"I don't know," Charlie said.

"Did he have enemies?" another wanted to know.

"I don't know," Charlie said.

"Did he ever have any dealings with Jonah Barnes?" a third shouted.

"I don't know. I don't know. I don't know!" Charlie said.

"When did you last see your ex-husband?"

"Repent. And sin no more," Paula Swenson's followers began marching around the corpse, widening their circle to include Charlie. "Let the sinner claim the sin," the marchers shouted.

"Let the beavers swim again!" the environmentalists chanted, holding their placards in the air.

Margaret and Paddy Murphy's mutt howled. The eagle launched from its tree, then glided south over the Great River Road where the Rev. Paula Swenson sped away in Spence Wood's Lexus.

94

Mary Swander's latest book is a co-edited collection of essays called The Healing Circle: Authors Writing of Recovery *(Plume, 1998). She is a professor of English at Iowa State University and lives in Ames and Kalona, Iowa, where she raises sheep and goats and a large organic vegetable garden.*

9

Watch Your Back

by Robley Wilson

In Des Moines, a couple of hundred miles removed from the maiden voyage of *La Bella*, Wild Bill Watson had come back from lunch to his *Register* cubicle— just in time to encounter a ringing telephone. Problem one was to find the damned phone; Watson's office was a clutter of books and papers, overflowing In and Out baskets, corrugated take-out boxes stained with grease, tomato sauce, brittle strands of cheese from pizza deliveries. It was hard enough to find his computer keyboard, especially since Sophie Brill, the arts editor, had started letting review copies of bad novels spill over into his territory.

He pushed aside a pile of magazines and bound galleys, found the phone, grabbed it.

"Yes," he yelled. "What?"

"Bill? Barry Bullyard here."

Watson settled into his desk chair and leaned back. "What a marvelous pleasure," he said in mock sweetness. "To what do we owe this unexpected contact?"

"Just thought I'd check in. I was having a late lunch—"

Watson exploded.

"Bullflap," he shouted, "what are you up to? What

are we paying you for? In what hole are you sticking your fingers today? I go out for a calm bite to eat and what do I see on the TV above the bar but the surprising news that there's not one, but TWO bodies washed up on the pristine beaches of Bella, Iowa, and I haven't heard one effing word about this second turn of events. Not from Charlie Andropolous, my usually reliable stringer, and not even from my alleged crackerjack reporter Barry Bumbling Bullcrap. Are you with the paper? Are you for us or against us?"

"Hey, keep your shirt on," Bullyard said. "We're a morning paper, remember? My deadline's hours away, and believe me, you wouldn't want this crazy story until it settles down into something readable."

Watson took a deep breath. No sense piling up any more anecdotal evidence to support his nickname.

"Look," he said, "it's okay to make the readers wait, but not the editors. Tell me what's happening."

"Well, Oprah's here with a crew—her first appearance in Iowa since her Madison County Embarrass-Your-Spouse show—and she's in one of her svelte phases, I might add. *The New York Times* has a couple of staffers here, words and pictures and look down your nose at the yokels. The Chicago papers are out in force, taking brewery tours for the most part. You've got a couple of blue-haired old ladies wired for Christmas lighting, a local police chief who might pass a driver's test if you didn't ask him to parallel park, a county sheriff with a German accent, a Jap moviemaker with no accent at all, and a local hairdresser who sat briefly at the bar with me while I ate lunch and she swilled a glass of whisky. You've also got a couple of hundred wild-eyed gamblers who are presently scarfing up free booze and raining quarters into any slot that presents itself. And that reminds me—"

"Sounds like you're having too much fun at the *Register's* expense. Reminds you of what?"

"That an ex-prosty named Pastor Paula Swenson has absconded with a luxury car—a tan Lexus—belonging to one of the dead men. And by the way, don't be too tough on your lady stringer. The dead car-owner turns out to be her husband."

"My God," Bill Watson said. "Poor Charlie."

"The other corpse was tied in with Pastor Prosty— fellow name of Jonah Barnes, rumored to have sprung the lady from a cathouse in Reno, set her up in some sort of lunatic-fringe religion, then embezzled the collection plate to the tune of plenty."

"How'd these guys get it?"

"Barnes was a single gunshot, close range, no sign of struggle. Mr. Charlie—Spence Wood by name— nobody's saying. The town of Bella's a bit small to support a coroner, so if the cause of death ain't obvious, you don't get a cause. My guess is he drowned in the Father of Waters, but don't quote me. Oh, and somebody'd tied a brick to his ankle."

"So the corpse would sink?"

"As if," Bullyard said. "I raised the question of suicide, but they tell me Wood was well-off, and he stood to make money off the riverboat deal—his law firm did a lot of the wheeling and dealing here. They do say Charlie was divorcing him—I hear they had a big blowup across the breakfast table this morning— but the split seems to have been mostly an amicable arrangement."

"What else?"

"Well, this might interest you. Another guy who's here for the big show is Lawrence Thomas, some fancy factotum in the holding company that bought the gambling rights locally."

Watson tapped the phone mouthpiece with his fingers, frowning, pondering. "Is that Larry Thomas? Slick Larry?"

"Might be."

"Wasn't he mixed up in that racetrack operation that fell apart a few years back?"

"Now you're cooking," Bullyard said. "You see why I'm letting things cool down a tad before I file the story. Too many threads to follow. I don't want to jump to any wrong conclusions."

"But how do you read it?" Watson wanted to know. "Off the record. Who's your prime suspect?"

"Maybe the reformed reverend. Stealing the Lexus was a screwy move, especially since she was supposed to be leading today's big antigambling demonstration."

"That didn't come off?"

"Who noticed? Anyway, she's at the top of everybody's list. Followed by Thomas—he's been running around with a pair of binoculars like he was Big Brother. And even your stringer herself; it wouldn't be the first crime of passion in a small Midwestern town. Or maybe this is going to be one of those Agatha Christie plots where the murderer is the last actor left standing."

"Then you'd better watch your back," Watson said.

"But you know," Bullyard said, "there've been a heck of a lot of dead beavers floating around the riverside. My guess is the authorities might learn as much from autopsying the beavers as they will from cutting open the humans."

"Very funny, Bullturd," Watson said. "Let's stick to common sense, shall we?"

"Whatever you say, o wildman. You'll find me right here at Joe's Bar & Grille. Every rumor in town either starts here or ends here, and I've got pencils behind both ears."

Pastor Paula ditched the Lexus at a McDonald's in Moline—left it in the parking lot behind a utility shed, used the facilities to wash her face and comb her hair, then strolled across the highway to a Citgo station with an outdoor phone booth. She used the calling card belonging to the Open Word Church of the Lord in the Woods by the River and dialed a number upriver in Bella.

A man's gruff voice answered: "Yeah. Who's this?"

"This Larry?"

A pause. Then, grudgingly, "Yeah, it's Larry. Who wants to know?"

"It's Paula, you creep. Who'd you think?"

"Listen: they're after you. They're looking for the car."

"I know that. What do you think I am—stupid?"

"Baby," Larry Thomas said—his voice had gone

sweeter—"where are you?"

"That's for me to know. What are you planning to do now?"

"Baby Doll. I don't know what you mean."

"Jonah's dead."

"Yeah, I saw that on the news. Shame."

"And so is Spence."

"I believe I heard that too."

"So?"

"It's been a violent and unusual day," Thomas said. "It rather takes the edge off the *La Bella*'s maiden voyage."

"You know what I mean, you jerk. I mean: what are you going to do to protect me?"

"I didn't know you needed protection, Baby Doll."

"Stop playing dumb; we've got cops for that. We're all in this together, and I for one want OUT."

Thomas didn't respond.

"You hear me, asshole?"

She heard Thomas chuckling.

"Well," he said, "you can take the broad out of the cathouse, but you can't take the cathouse out of the broad."

"Screw you," said Pastor Paula. "I need money, and you're the one's got to send it to me."

"Where are you, Baby?"

"I'm in Moline."

"What are you doing in Moline?"

"I'm taking a tour of John Deere's," Paula said. "What do you think?"

"And why should I send you money?"

"Because I know where all the bodies are buried,"

Paula said. "I know names, and places, and amounts."

There was a momentary silence on the line. Then: "You don't know squat," Thomas said.

"I know who the three sisters are," Paula told him. "I know Anne and Charlotte and Emily, and I know what their initials spell, and it isn't BARF."

"So what?"

"And I know what Spence was after when he doubled back to the B & B this morning, and I know why you were both staying there, and I by God know the names of the people in Chicago who're backing you."

Silence on the other end of the line.

"You hearing me?" Paula said. "You LISTENING to me?" More silence. Then, Larry:

"What are you asking me to do?"

"Pay attention," she said. "I've still got the church credit card, so I can get plane tickets. I'm heading out to Reno, and I'll need cash when I get there. Wire the money to Momma Sanders at the old Mustang Ranch, where you and Jonah first knew me."

"How much?"

"What's your skin worth?"

"There ain't that much money in the world, Baby Doll. Tell me how much."

"Five thousand," Paula said. "And that's just a down payment."

A long pause.

"You got it," Larry Thomas said at last.

She hung up the phone. From a side pocket of her purse she drew out a bank card. It would get her a cab to the airport, a ticket to Reno via St. Louis, a motel room when she arrived.

"VISA. It's everywhere you want to be," she repeated to herself. But where on earth was that?

102   Barry Bullyard had moved his base of operations. He was no longer at the fake-mahogany bar in the dim interior of Joe's, but had moved to a booth in the back corner of the place. He was not alone. Alongside him sat Floyd Delmer, the county supervisor who had told the world what a "cash cow" the gambling boat would be. Across from him was Paddy Murphy, the innkeeper who'd worked hand-in-glove with Spence Wood as the *La Bella* arrangements were being made, and "Ken the Nip"—as Barry had christened him this afternoon—with his notebook and his inscrutable face and his handycam on the floor between his feet.

It was evening; the *La Bella* had long been back at its pier to let ashore those who wanted an onshore dinner, and it was already on the river again, cruising southward with fresh gambling fools aboard. Joe's was overrun with the afternoon crowd, drinking too much too fast, and regaling the room with their wins and losses on the riverboat's maiden cruise.

Barry's interests had nothing to do with wins and losses. Instead, he was buying rounds for his newfound companions and trying to ask the right questions, hoping the answers would make the story he was obliged to send on to his editor before his ten o'clock deadline.

"And how long had this so-called Brother Jonah lived in Bella?" was one of his questions, but what he'd got from the assembled guests was a blank look and a polite shrug.

"Well," Floyd Delmer allowed, "if memory serves, old J. Barnes was a second-rate salesman of some sort."

"Pharmaceuticals," said Paddy Murphy.

"What's that?"

"Drugs, in other words," Paddy repeated.

"That's my understanding," said Ken the Nip. "Pink pills for pale people."

He looked around and grinned.

"That lets me out," he said.

"You're pale enough," Delmer said. "Don't flatter yourself you're so goddamn different from us Caucasians."

"What's all this?" Barry wondered out loud.

"Hell, don't mind him," Paddy said. "Just his old man landed on Okinawa back in '45. Floyd here's still fighting the war in the Pacific."

"Am not," Floyd said.

"Are too," said Paddy. "You're like a broken record."

"Or a blemished CD," Ken said.

Floyd scowled and turned his beer glass between his palms. "Just I never seen a Japanese looked less like a Japanese than this guy. Whatsisname."

"Ken," Ken said.

Floyd shook his head. "Doesn't sound to me like any kind of Nip name."

"Me neither," Paddy agreed, "if the truth be known."

"So what are you saying?" Barry asked the two locals. "Are you accusing Ken of something? Of trying to be something he really isn't?"

"Right," Ken said. "If I'm not me, then who am I? I'd really like to be the first to know."

"Very funny," Floyd said. "Very effing funny."

Ken grinned and leaned back against the vinyl cushion of the booth. He winked at Barry.

There you go, thought Barry; he imagines we're blood brothers because we're both reporters—him with his documentaries, me with my columns. What a nerve. He was about to say this—What a nerve!— when the door to Joe's swung open and Poor Ellen Gutcheon stood silhouetted in the light of the setting sun.

"Where's the chief of police?" she said plaintively. "Where's the sheriff?"

Paddy Murphy was already halfway to the door. "What is it, Ellen? What's the matter?"

"It's that nice man staying at the Three Sisters, Mr. Thomas. He looks to have fallen out of an upstairs window. He's lying flat on his face in the driveway. I think he's broken his neck."

Good God, thought Barry Bullyard, how can you file a story when the facts of it change every time you take a breath? The corpses kept piling up. It was like being in the last act of *Hamlet*.

Floyd Delmer sighed audibly. "One damned thing after another," he said. "And poor dear Ellen." He watched the woman as she repeated her story for the bar's other patrons, then turned to Barry. "Nice hair though," he said.

Robley Wilson has taught at UNI since 1963. He is the author of a novel, four story collections, and two poetry collections. He has edited The North American Review *since 1968.*

10

The Fat Man

by Greg Shanley

Paddy Murphy snuck out of Joe's. He regretted that decision almost immediately. Inside, he was surrounded by friends and acquaintances; outside, he was alone and vulnerable. But Paddy was an action guy, always had been. He learned early in life, growing up the son of a teacher and a nurse, that problems did not disappear on their own. He was not sure why, but he could not stand to have unresolved problems hanging over his head. And make no mistake, this was a doozy! The three people he had worked most closely with to bring riverboat gambling to Bella were dead, all apparently murdered, and a fourth person who was part of their little group had fled town suspiciously in Spence's car.

Paddy did not feel guilty about bringing riverboat gambling to Bella. He believed it would cause cash to pour into the tiny community which could help improve schools and the city's infrastructure. As a result of those positive changes, other businesses might decide Bella was just the sort of place they wanted to be. However, he did regret the games he and the leaders of the boat supporters group used to manipulate the rest of Bella's residents.

The biggest trick was Pastor Paula. She was in the

hip pocket of the boat supporters from the beginning. Spence and Jonah came up with that plan when they met in Nevada a few years ago and learned they had more in common than just living in Bella. Each was hooked on Paula. It was easy to convince the other members of their not-so-secret group that there was no better or surer way to win a tough political battle than have the opposition unknowingly led by a key supporter. Even though it was devious, Paddy had to admit it was ingenious. The opposition was never allowed to grow too big. If it ever threatened to gain critical mass, Pastor Paula would pretend to be fanatical, go over the edge, and push many antigambling activists out of the organized effort. Once gone, they lacked money, were generally ignored, and eventually became silent out of frustration.

Was Pastor Paula really a murderer? Paddy didn't think so. Yes, she was a whore. Yes, she was very good at her job, and yes, she was greedy. However, that did not add up to murder. But why did she run? Was she running from someone? Paddy hoped she would contact him soon. With Jonah Barnes, Spence Wood, and Larry Thomas all dead there was no one else for her to contact.

He entered his yard through the alley, simultaneously stumbling over a sprinkler and swearing. Paddy had trouble finding his house key. He kept all his work-related keys on one ring and his personal keys on another. In the dark it was a chore to distinguish between the two. After a few more seconds and more swearing he found the right key and started to put it in the lock, but the door was open and freely swung in.

The place had been dismantled. Nothing was in one piece. Even the porcelain bathtub and toilet had been shattered. Paddy collapsed in the middle of what used to be his living room. He thought to himself that he had to sort this mess out, and he was not thinking about dirty dishes. He tried mentally to focus on the riverboat, its maiden voyage, and three dead people.

109

Barry Bullyard was just getting ready to feed his story to his editor. Bullyard said it looked like these murders might have legs for weeks. "Legs" was newspaper lingo for a gold mine of stories. Bullyard pressed a few key buttons on his laptop and away it went. He sure liked feeding stories this way. In the old days, the editors would be harassing you all the while you were dictating a story. This way, they generally read the thing top to bottom and started cutting before they started hollering for sections to be rewritten.

The thrust of the story was three murders surrounding the maiden voyage of Bella's riverboat, with a local pastor the only suspect. Wild Bill Watson asked if Bullyard had seen Charlie since Spence's murder. Bullyard said he saw her from a distance, but she was too upset to approach at the time. He said he planned to stop at the Three Sisters in the morning on the way to a news conference at City Hall. Bullyard was not expecting to get much new information. He speculated the Chief was looking for television exposure. With three murders in Bella, reporters from Iowa's largest cities would hit town like locusts in the morning.

Watson hung up with Bullyard and contemplated calling Charlie. He knew she had suffered through one of the worst days anyone could imagine, and he needed to express his condolences and make sure she understood she was off this story. He hesitated making the call because he knew she was going to fight him, but he was not going to back down. If ever there was a clear example of a conflict of interest this was it!

Charlie was groggy. She was stuck between reality and her dreams, and a strong valium was pulling her back toward the dream. She struggled to a semi-wakeful state and picked up the phone, but before she could say anything she heard "This is Ken." Then another voice said, "The fat man smokes a cigar in the morning and the fat woman exhales!"

Charlie was wide awake now. She heard a click, and she quickly hung up wondering what the hell that was all about. Ken? He seemed the only one without a connection to all the craziness in Bella. Now she did not know what to think. She leaned back and tried to focus on the events of the past few days, but the valium and stress overtook her and she was quickly asleep.

Ken was distressed. He was positive he had heard a second click. Who had heard the message? Did they hear the whole thing? At what point did they pick it up? Ken felt foolish using phony voices and clandestine messages, but they usually proved their worth. This was a perfect example. Even though someone may have heard the message, they would have no idea what it meant, so his cover was still useful. He turned off the light, turned on his right side and decided he needed some sleep because tomorrow was going to be a busy day.

The next morning Dixie was downstairs making breakfast for those guests at the Three Sisters that were still breathing. She was muttering about giving everyone some Captain Crunch, but at the same time she was mixing ingredients for a Western omelet. Ken came down, grabbed a couple of bagels, bid everyone a good day and scurried away saying something about filming a local master canoe maker.

Charlie came down a few minutes later and was disappointed Ken had already left. She had made up her mind to be direct and ask just what the hell was going on? That would have to wait.

Barry Bullyard blew in the front door and told her how sorry he was for everything happening around her. She graciously accepted and asked him to sit down and join them for breakfast. He eagerly accepted the invitation.

Charlie said, "Wild Bill called me this morning and was very supportive and kind, but he took me off the story. He was so nice I just couldn't bring myself to argue. But just because I'm not working for the *Register* doesn't mean I'm going to stop my investigation."

Barry thought that was a huge mistake, but he

kept quiet, wolfed down his omelet, thanked them, and told them he had to leave to make the news conference.

"So many reporters are expected, the chief's decided to hold it in the city council chambers," he told them.

Charlie was crushed she could not go, but she did not want to face questions from the other reporters about Spence's death. Dixie perked up and said there was no reason she could not go. The council chambers were public property and there was no legal way they could keep her out.

Dixie arrived about five minutes early. There had to be about 50 reporters present. She recognized several television reporters.

Police Chief John Lawless approached the microphone, cleared his throat and said, "I have a statement to make. I want to assure everyone that Bella is a safe community. No tourists has received as much as a scratch and none will as long as I'm in charge! We have had three recent deaths, and at this time we are treating each of them as suspicious in nature. I'll now try and answer any questions you might have."

Barry Bullyard sat quietly. He was not about to tip any other reporters to the information he had gathered over the past few days. He had learned the hard way that questions at news conferences can give clues to his competitors. Barry looked around and saw all the usual print and broadcast reporters who got assigned to these stories. He couldn't help but notice

Oprah. He wondered what she was doing here since she had made a real effort to be uplifting in her show. What was going on in Bella was hardly uplifting!

Barry thought the Police Chief had not embarrassed himself too much so far, but he knew the real test was coming. No hands shot up, but everyone tried to get their question in first by shouting. They finally backed down to the loudest voice in the throng.

"Is there a serial killer on the loose in Bella?"

The Chief said, "I do not have enough evidence to tie the three apparent murders together."

"Have you determined a motive for these murders?"

"I cannot release that information at this time."

"Is Pastor Paula a suspect?"

"She is wanted for questioning. I would not call her a suspect at this time."

"But Chief, she fled the scene in Spence Wood's car! What do you have to do to be a suspect in this town?"

Scattered snickers spread across the room.

"Chief, I see some Department of Criminal Investigation Agents behind you. Who is in charge here?"

Looking like a deer in headlights the Chief replied, "This is my case."

"What help is the DCI offering?"

"Just what I ask for, although they already had an agent in town keeping an eye on the riverboat and all associated activities."

Barry Bullyard's ears perked up. Then he blurted out, "Are you saying the DCI has an undercover agent here?"

An angry looking DCI agent stepped forward and said, "This case will not be investigated in the media. If we have an agent undercover in Bella, I assure you we would never compromise their safety by discussing their duties while they are still investigating a case. At least we haven't until now!" He shot the Chief a menacing look and concluded the news conference with, "Thank you all for coming."

As Barry Bullyard stepped outside and stretched, he saw Oprah and her crew piling into a limo. He overheard her say, "This is a waste of time. I'm not going back to covering this gory stuff just because I happened to be here when these murders occurred. There is some very bad karma here. I can't wait to catch the next plane back to Chicago. I need to cleanse my soul. I hope Maya Angelou is home; I could use some of her spiritual guidance."

Greg Shanley was raised in a suburb of Cleveland, Ohio. He has worked as a broadcast journalist in Florida, North Carolina and Texas. He moved to Iowa and began working at KUNI in 1986 where he is currently news director. He has won numerous state, regional and national broadcast journalism awards.

This is the second book for KUNI for which he has served as project director. The first book was Moments In Iowa History, *published in 1997. He is not related to Mary Kay Shanley.*

11

Sin No More

by Cynthia Mercati

Bella's "misguided missionary," the antigambling savior, the diva of the airwaves, the foremost Bible thumping, lectern pounding, sin selling, salvation proclaiming, redemption purveyor Iowa had ever produced, Pastor Paula herself, raised a shot glass of Jack Daniels and toasted herself.

"Nice work, girl!"

She tossed down the thick amber liquid. Pastor Paula had a whole row of shot glasses marching down the red plastic tablecloth that covered the cheap, scarred table that sat right smack in the middle of Guido's Country Bar, and now she picked up another one and made another toast to herself.

"Nice mess you got yourself into!"

She downed the glass, then she picked up a fork and stabbed some of the french fries laying at the bottom of the red napkined basket containing the remnants of her Guido Special. But a tenderloin and fries couldn't do what Jack Daniels did, never had. She downed another shot and made another toast.

"You are one fine piece of work, girl!"

She hoisted another glass, and slurred her way through another toast. "To you, Spence. I don't know if I loved you, but it sure felt like it." Paula turned her head toward the bar, where half a dozen bearded, long-haired construction workers were downing their after work beers and not even trying to talk.

"Hey!" she called out. "Why don't one of you play something sweet and sad on the jukebox, something a woman can cry to."

One of the men dislodged himself from the bar stool, hitching up his pants over his formidable belly, and ambled toward the jukebox.

"How 'bout Hank Williams?" he asked.

Paula nodded.

"Perfect, as long as it's Hank Williams, Sr. and not that souless son of his."

In a minute "I'm Walking the Floor over You" was playing. Paula downed another shot and talked to herself—or rather, to Spence, even though he was long past hearing.

"You were one in a million, Spence," she said softly. She hiccupped, wiped her mouth on the back of her hand and went on. "I know you were a bounder and a rounder and a player and a gamer, but hell, you made me feel—special."

She nodded to herself and sniffed back a tear. "Yep, you made me feel special, that's what you did." She knew she was getting sloppy drunk and hated herself for it, but she couldn't help it. She knew Spence had been playing her for a fool most of the time, and pulling the wool over her eyes the rest of the time, but she didn't care. Spence had this kind of magic he could work on women, find their weakness, discover what it was they needed most, and give it to them. It worked everytime, and she was no exception. Oh, Lordy, had it worked with her. When she was with Spence, no-good, heartbreakin', good lookin' devil that he was, she'd felt delicate and sweet and innocent! Wasn't that a laugh. She'd felt innocent. Like it was her first time. She'd felt cherished. Her, Paula Swenson, former lowlife hooker, dope smokin' high school dropout runaway, had felt cherished.

And in her way, she'd cherished him, too—only her feelings had been for real. But she'd never been able to penetrate the mask Spence wore, never once. What was he really, she'd often wondered, and wondered too, if he'd known himself. Every time he'd left her, she'd asked herself the same question: Who was he, really? And what did he want? Once in a while, she could get a glimpse of the man behind that well-constructed mask, and what she saw was a glimmer of fear. The fear of giving a chunk of himself away, of maybe actually needing someone.

Paula suspected that bird-watching, cake-baking, casserole-making Charlie-the-Innkeeper had come as close as anyone to being let into Spence's private world. Paula suspected he might even have loved Charlie, in his own way. But not even Charlie, she was sure, knew all there was to know about the man,

"Hell," Paula said aloud, "I bet she didn't know a quarter of what the man was, 'cause if Spence ever suspected he was getting too fond of that apron-wearing, batter-stirring, griddle-washin' gal, he would have been scared out of his wits—so scared he would have turned and run."

And maybe that's just what he had been doing. Or trying to do when he got caught. Got caught one last time. And now Barnes was gone . . . and Lawrence . . . and Spence. And she'd known them all and loved one, and was with them in their scam deeper than a donut in dung. Three down—and more to go?

Paula jumped to her feet, shaking suddenly, her stomach turning and tumbling. More to go. She should be on the plane to Nevada. She should be outta here. She should be a gone girl. She sat down again, smiling. She should be alotta things she wasn't and never had been. Hell, she had time for one more drink. One last toast. She lifted a glass.

"To what was, what was gonna be—and ain't." Prior to coming into Guido's, Paula had headed herself into the Moline outlet store for Frederick's of Hollywood and carried into the dressing room an outfit that reminded her of the good old days at the Mustang Ranch: a micromini black silk skirt with a slit, black fishnet tights, black stiletto heels, and an off-the-shoulder red silk top. She would have added a rose in her teeth if she could have found one, 'cause she was celebrating the demise of Pastor Paula's Midwest, middle class frumpiness. After charging it all on her Divine Word credit card, Paula had found her way behind the store and bunching up her navy blue blazer and skirt—reaching two inches below the knee, of course—the burgundy blouse with the Peter Pan collar, and the low heeled pumps, she'd stuffed them into the dumpster with a shout of freedom.

Yep, it was back to the old life, and if it wasn't exactly the good life, it was a life a lot more honest than the one she'd been leading in Bella. She downed another shot.

"Sin floats and don't I know it!" Paula proclaimed loudly, and thought how much she'd relish having the whole of Bella and especially those thin-lipped, tight-assed, holier-than-thou hypocrites that made up her congregation, see her now.

Suddenly, she remembered Charlie's question to her. "What are you doing here?"

What was I doing there, she wondered now. What was I doing with those losers? What have I been doing anywhere . . . ever?

She needed to snap out of this funk. This fear. This feeling of having lost the love of her life and the deal of her life, and the rest of her life. She stood, set one high heel on the chair, then another, and then was standing on the table, hands on her hips. She put both hands to her mouth and blew. One thing she could always do was make an earsplitting whistle, and time hadn't lessened her talent.

The men at the bar, the bartender, the surly waitress with the blonde hair like straw, even Guido himself, lounging against the back wall, all snapped to attention.

"Come on, "Paula yelled. "We're gonna have a hymn sing!"

"The hell we are!" the bottle blonde waitress yelled out.

"The hell we is!" the beer-bellied man who had plugged the jukebox shouted back, and the other drinkers all agreed.

"Fat lotta tips I'm gonna get outta that," the waitress sulked and slammed her way out to the kitchen.

"Okay!" Paula shouted. "Are you with me?"

"You bet we are, little lady," one of the men shouted back.

They started to clap their hands. A long-haired mountain man type in a tye-dyed T-shirt called out "What we gonna sing first?"

"The Little Brown Church in the Vale!" Paula answered back. It had always been a personal favorite and one she could always get her congregation rocking with. Well, as much as that uptight bunch of stiff-necked folks rocked. She lifted both arms high and started in. The men joined her. Some people off the street, intrigued by the noise, pushed open the door and joined in. Then some more. Soon the place was full.

"Okay!" Paula said, pointing to the group at the bar. "You do the COME, COME, COME part! You folks at the tables, you do the COME TO THE CHURCH IN THE WILD WOOD! part. Let's see who's the loudest! Ready, set, go!"

They followed that song with *Rock of Ages*, which made the tye-dyed man cry, and then went into *Blessed Assurance*, finishing with *Onward Christian Soldiers* which ended with everyone on their feet and just about ready to march down the main drag of Moline and pull sinners in by the scruff of their necks.

"You're a great bunch of singers," Paula yelled enthusiastically, "and a great big bunch of sinners, too, I bet!"

"You bet right!" the juke box jockey called out,

and then everyone was clapping and drinking and feeling real good about themselves. Now Paula started to dance to a handclapping rhythm of her own, which was taken up by everyone in the place. She started singing a song, too, of her own design. "Hey, hey, repent and sin no more! Let the sinner claim the sin!" She grabbed someone's drink and chugged it and sang a few more improvised words, still dancing, "Repent and sin no more, no more! Repent and sin no more!" She finished on a big fat crescendo. "And let the beavers swim again, Oh, yes let the beavers swim againnnn!"

Paula finished with her hands up over her head, her skirt halfway to kingdom come and everybody having a heck of a wonderful time. Flushed and grinning, Paula sat down at her table again, pleased with herself. Yep, it was true. You could take the girl out of the pulpit, but you couldn't—well, however that saying went, it was true. She hadn't lost her touch. She was still good for more than a few laughs. Yep, the old Paula was still there, jumping and jiving and kicking and singing and swinging. And that old Paula should just get up and get outta here, and head on down Nevada way.

Of course there was still that big fat old mess she was up to her eyeballs in. She should clean that up first, start with a clean slate. Or should she? After all, she'd cut out on messes before. None as bad or as big as this one, of course, but then you never knew what the future held. If she lit out now, she might just latch on to something—or someone—bigger and better than what she'd had going in Bella.

She made a small noise of despair. A bigger and better someone the future might indeed hold, but no matter who he was, he wouldn't be Spence . . .

Guido oiled up to her. "Hey, I like your style."

"I like yours too," Paula answered, without missing a beat. He was a head shorter than she was, with big pores and arms like ham slabs, but what the heck, he was still a man. And she still knew all the right words. All the right moves.

"Yeah, I like your style, girl. How 'bout coming to work for me?"

"What would I do?"

"What you just did! Liven the place up a little, start sing-alongs, jump up on tables—oh, and when you get a minute, take orders."

Paula smiled knowingly. "You mean you want a waitress."

Guido laughed. "Among other things."

"Well, Mister Guido, I just might consider it." She patted his arm and he covered her hand with his own. Paula stared at the big, hairy knuckles, at his big lips, smacking now in anticipation. Sure I'll consider it, Paula thought, when pigs fly.

Guido winked at her. "You do that, honey." He went off whistling. A waitress at Guido's. It could be a hoot. For about five minutes. She better get her hide back to the Mustang Ranch while she was still in one piece. The Ranch had been like a haven before, a home almost. The only one she'd ever really known. She pulled out her credit card and looked at it, the little piece of plastic that for the moment could still get her wherever she wanted to be. But where on earth was that?

It wasn't where she'd been born, that was for sure. And it wasn't where she'd just been. Maybe she should try somewhere new as someone new. Maybe she should try to pass herself off as a rich, sophisticated, jet setting beautiful person. A widow. Yeah, that was it. A beautiful rich widow, kind of like Jackie O. Or, like Princess Di, only a little older and alive. Yeah, she'd dump the bimbo getup and go for the classic look, maybe a suit and cigarette holder. Yeah, that sounded good.

But how long could she bring it off? There'd she be, sipping champagne on the Riviera, and in her mind she'd start hearing a Tanya Tucker song—she felt like a soulmate to Tanya Tucker—and she'd be dancing on tables again. It'd be even harder to be a rich, classy widow than a pastor, because as strict as Preacher Paula was supposed to be, when she started spitting brimstone and spouting off about sin and such, she could work up to a good ole frenzy, and get everyone else all heated up, too. She doubted that rich, classy widows like Jackie O. ever got down and dirty. If the urge to get wild overtook 'em, they probably just went shopping. No, she better make tracks to the Mustang Ranch. On the double.

But what about here? What about the what and the who she was leaving behind? Or trying to. What had she told Larry Thomas? She knew where the bodies were buried? She did indeed, and now Jonah Barnes was deader than a doornail. And Spence.

Her Spence. No, never that. But he had been the

man she loved. But if she stayed in Iowa, how would she ever come through what was waiting for her? If she stayed, she'd have to fight, but then, she'd always been a fighter. Even when she was a snot-nosed kid, running loose on the streets. The only one she'd never been able to fight was her mean-as-sin father, who'd beat her and tried to bed her. She couldn't fight him, so she'd run. She hadn't wanted to fight her Mama. There was nothing to fight in Mama. She'd been drained of life long ago, with nary a word to say for herself unless it was Sunday morning, when for an hour or two, the preacher gave her a glimmer of hope.

Paula smiled. If only Mama could have seen her wayward daughter behind the pulpit, she would finally have been proud of her.

Paula's head jerked up. Because Ken had suddenly strolled into Guido's. Nonchalant Ken, smiling that smile that never reached his eyes and never gave anything away.

He reached her table.

"Have you heard?" he asked her. "The fat man smokes a cigar in the morning and the fat woman exhales."

Beneath her heavy make-up, Paula went white.

Cynthia Mercati is the author of 30 published plays as well as three novels, and numerous stories, articles, and commentary. She was born and bred in Chicago—definitely a city girl—but several of her latest plays have had Iowa themes. Grant Wood: Prairie Rebel *is currently touring the state, and* Tell Me The Story of Iowa *was written for the Sesquicentennial celebration.*

12

Madness All Around

by Larry Erickson

In a corner of the Three Sisters Bed and Breakfast Inn, Charlie sat at her desk, sorting through random papers and feelings. She had always loved her little office, a cheery alcove of floral print paper framed by dark Victorian woodwork. She and Spence had fixed the squeaky floors in the guest rooms, pounding shims around joists and driving screws everywhere. But here in her office, Charlie had tried to explain to him that she found some kind of inspiration in the old inn's creaks and groans. Spence had thought her silly, but that was part of her charm— and it meant less work for them both, he had said.

She covered her mouth with a trembling hand, hiding her lips as they shaped his name again and again.

"Spence, Spence, Spence . . ."

The memory of restoring the inn was real and warm, and she clung to it briefly. But it wasn't enough to block the cold and unreal image of his muddy and bloody body twisted along the edge of the river where gentle waves lapped grotesquely against his side.

Trying to escape that image, Charlie stroked the sleek shoulder of their Boston bulldog.

"Glad you're back," she murmured to Margaret,

who looked up appreciatively. Dogs are such sympathetic friends, Charlie thought, grateful that the dog had turned up along the river after being absent from the inn all day. Charlie suspected that Spence may have had Margaret along when he disappeared and that Margaret had been looking for his killer.

Charlie turned again to shuffling papers without purpose, stacking and cleaning, searching for distractions rather than documents. She had been gripped by shock, running on emotional autopilot since Spence's body was found. Now reality was taking hold, shaking her soul, and the papers rustled in her trembling hands.

Some kid at the *Register* state desk had left a voice mail yesterday, when Bella was still sane, saying he'd faxed a list of riverboat details that Bill Watson would need. Now, on top of everything else, the fax wasn't working. It didn't really matter now, but Charlie was furious and the fax machine offered a target for rage. She muttered to herself about Ken, who had been using the inn's cluttered little office even more than she had during the past week.

A telltale creak foretold the arrival of someone in the hall as Margaret whined and pressed closer to Charlie's ankle.

"How's it going there, kiddo?" Dixie asked as she came into the room and dropped heavily into the other chair. The answer was obvious. "Look, nobody's expecting you to work today, not as an innkeeper and certainly not as a reporter. Besides, you're too close to this story . . ."

"But that's why I've got to do this," Charlie exploded. "Who ever heard of Dan Rather before he got the network's attention when Kennedy was shot in Dallas? I've got to . . . Spence would expect me to do something, wouldn't he, Dix?" she asked, her voice choking. "I'm really trying—but he's dead, and I can't even get the damn fax machine to work."

Overwhelmed and overwrought, Charlie covered her face with her hands and sobbed.

"OK, this part I can help with," Dixie said, stroking her friend's head gently. "Look, I had trouble with this thing last week. See, it stores the most recent faxes in a memory, like a computer. So if it's out of paper or out of sorts, you don't lose messages. Here, you just push this button twice, then type in the code . . . "

The fax machine responded with a series of electro-chirps, its thin message panel registered "RECYCL MEM," then its printer started to hum. It spewed out the missing list of questions from the editor's office, a previous menu request from a recent guest at the inn, a budget report from Ken's production company, and a page that looked like the end of a letter.

Dixie was drawn to the letter's bold and totally illegible scrawl of a signature. While Charlie looked over the sheet from the newspaper, Dixie absently studied the other pages.

"Dix, that's got to be more of Ken's stuff. He's been using this office more than . . . "

A sharp gasp from Dixie stopped Charlie in mid-sentence. "What?"

"Charlie . . . look at this!"

They squeezed shoulder-to-shoulder as they read, the letter held between them like a hymnal. The page started in mid-paragraph, talking routinely about television demographics and cable markets. Then, it read:

> *"You know we're damned serious about this, Ken. We're not about to sponsor another sugary travelogue that nobody watches. That audience disappeared long ago, just like your career is going to disappear unless you show some initiative on this project. You know the figures on the tabloid shows as well as I do: Sex sells. Crime sells.*
>
> *You're the one who told me about the drug traffic in Iowa. You said organized crime is tied to the gambling there. And you said the law may be on the take. Now I expect you to deliver and the partners expect us to deliver! I don't care what kind of sappy country backdrop you shoot for this project, but you get some action and some drama that we can take to the bank or I'm pulling the plug. Now get me something people will watch!"*

The signature looked like a swoosh followed by a zigzag from an electrocardiogram.

Charlie looked like she'd just seen another body.

"Charlie, you sit tight," Dixie said. "I'm going to hide this and then we're going to figure out what to do."

While Charlie slumped in her chair, clinging to Margaret, Dixie scuttled off toward the kitchen.

Armed with a glass of brandy, she took the letter to her room and closed the door. She sat at her dressing table, sighed heavily, and tossed back the brandy. As she felt the warmth of it spread through her chest, she slipped the letter under her mattress, next to the revolver.

Charlie caught herself hyperventilating and fought to control her own breathing.

"Good girl," she mumbled absently as Margaret sighed and settled into her lap. What kind of cruel twist is this, she wondered. She had planned such an idyllic life, so far from the madness of the world. And suddenly madness was all around her, like the tornados that tear up random lives in Iowa every summer. But this wasn't a random act of nature; this was the evil of human nature—and it was personal.

"We can't just hide until this blows over," she whispered to the dog. "And we can't trust anybody to save us."

Charlie grabbed a clean sheet of paper and penciled at the top "Suspects." Then she started listing everyone she could think of who might be connected to the deaths. She heard the hallway creak again.

"OK, Margaret, it's you and me and Dixie," she said, nuzzling the dog. "Dixie, we're going to solve this thing . . . " she started to say when Margaret bolted from her lap. Charlie was looking up toward the doorway when the familiar surroundings suddenly disappeared in a white light, followed by a sharp pain and slow, sickening darkness.

In Moline, Paula Swenson opened her eyes painfully. Less an awakening, really, than a gradual effort to focus on consciousness. Her body ached, her head throbbed, and she could feel tiny wads of cotton stuffed into every numbed cell of her brain. Slowly, through long blinks crusted with mascara, she brought the room into focus, a room she didn't recall. A motel room.

A searing shaft of sunlight burned through a slit between heavy curtains. Paula stared in dull fascination at the dust dancing in this thin sliver of a spotlight. It was obviously midday, but what day? In the shadows, Paula's vision took a vague inventory: a tacky dresser, a bolted-down TV that was turned on but without volume. In the blue flicker of television light, she saw a pile of silky fabric that looked only vaguely familiar. She focused on the clothing: cheesy red and black things, with more lace than style, more danger than promise . . .

A strained mask of anguished recollection spread over her face and she dropped her head back into the pillow.

"Oh, God," she whispered hoarsely. "Not again, not now, not this." On the nightstand next to her lay five crumpled $20 bills.

Larry Erickson writes magazine articles and edits do-it-yourself books for Meredith Corporation in Des Moines. He lives on a hobby farm near Adel, where he raises eyebrows.

13

Double Down

by Nancy K. Barry

The light stung her eyes and made her body come alert with an aching sensation, as if each limb were waking up, one by one, first with pain, and then with fear. Where was she, Charlie wondered, feeling as if she had lost her bearings completely. She lifted herself up by pulling hard on the oak chair, and once she was eye-level with the desk, realized that her small corner of private space in the alcove of the Three Sisters had been completely ransacked. File folders she didn't even know she had were strewn across the desk, their papers spilled out and mixed with the contents of the wire trash basket. Envelopes were torn open, canceled checks littered the floor like play money, and every drawer of the old Victorian desk was emptied into a heap.

Someone wanted something from her—or from the old house—and was willing to work pretty damn hard to get it. The events of the last two days were starting to look even more gothic than Charlie wanted, despite her namesake. Suddenly, she was seized by another fear, remembering the last thing she had done before the blinding dark pulled her under.

"Margaret," she called out anxiously, "Margaret— where are you? Dixie . . . Dixie are you here?"

The house answered back with an eerie silence. Charlie felt the adrenaline rise up her legs and into her chest, as she pushed back from the desk quietly, quickly realizing that whoever had knocked her out might have done the same to Dixie, or silenced the dog completely. Her throat tightened.

She took two tentative steps out from the alcove, and listened hard for any noises. Her mind raced back to what happened before she was knocked out, but could only remember the cryptic words of the phone message she had heard: "fat . . . cigar . . . exhales." What the hell was going on around here, she wondered, almost starting to giggle at the total absurdity of it all, until she heard the sounds coming from the kitchen downstairs.

She grabbed the only weapon she could find in the hallway, a decorated fireplace bellows hanging on the wall for decoration. She began tiptoeing down the steps, wincing at each creek they made in response, until she got closer to the kitchen and could sense the presence of another body. She knew every corner of this old house and when a stranger was breathing in it, she could tell. As she reached the final step, she peered into the kitchen and saw a man's frame staring out the window. She lifted the bellows back over her head, leaped out from the doorway, and whacked her suspect over the head with the tool. He fell to the floor more in shock than in pain, and Charlie saw to her distress the crane-like face of John Lawless twitching beneath her.

"Chief!" She exclaimed. "What are you doing here?" He started to get up, but Charlie stopped him. "Hold on," she said, "Just sit there a minute until you catch your breath." She began to pump the bellows to squirt air into his face, but only dust and soot came out the nozzle. Lawless starting coughing and wheezing, until Charlie handed him a glass of water in-between her apologies.

Slowly, Lawless pieced together an explanation. "Those two women with the sweatshirts that light up every time they win," he said. "They had come back to their rooms and found the place torn up and ransacked like a burglary. One of them, Doris, I think her name was, kept saying she thought it was just part of the deluxe package of the B & B, but the other one insisted they report it. I told them I would come over and check it out. You know, you really should keep that back door closed."

Charlie sighed, murmuring, "The brick we used found another calling."

Suddenly, John Lawless turned philosophical, asking in a small voice, "Charlie, how'd you get mixed up in all this, anyway?"

"Me," she wailed. "This has nothing to do with me, or Dixie. All I know is, we found a fax for Ken Whatshisname that suggested he wanted more out of this story than a sleepy Midwestern town. The next thing I know, I'm getting whacked over the head and someone has pulled the house apart like an old pillow." Saying her friend's name made Charlie seize up with fear again. "Wait a minute, where's Dixie?"

"We better find her," she added. "If another body

washes up anywhere near the Three Sisters, the health department's going to shut me down."

She pulled John Lawless to his feet and tried to plan a course of action, remembering the bizarre code phrase she had heard on the phone for Ken.

"Chief," she said, "Have you ever heard some phrase about a fat man smoking a cigar in the morning, and a fat woman exhaling?"

To John Lawless, such a phrase was just another in a long string of unknowns he couldn't even count on his fingers anymore. He listened while Charlie went through her own mental checklist surrounding the murders.

"My theory is, Larry Thomas, Jonah Barnes, and Spence must have been involved with some not-so-clean arrangements regarding the boat financing. Somehow, one or more of them got scared, or greedy, or both, and decided the only good partner was a dead partner."

"But why would Paula split?"

"Maybe she's not as crazy as we all thought."

"Are you saying Paula Swenson killed somebody?"

"I'm saying three out of four people involved in the harbor deal and the gambling boat are dead, and somebody wants something hidden somewhere to tell them something.

"Wait a minute," she continued. "Have you interviewed Paddy Murphy?" Before Lawless had time to answer, Charlie saw Margaret racing up the street, followed by Paddy Murphy's dog nipping along at her heels, trying to keep up. As soon as the dogs saw Charlie, they began to jump and bark crazily, as if they were desperate to tell her something. Charlie scooped up her pet and tried to calm it, but the mutt had another idea, racing back down the street towards Joe's.

Charlie and the Police Chief could only look at each other and run along with the dogs, taking their chances that the canines had more sense than anybody else in the town seemed to.

The dogs led them around the back entrance of the bar, toward a small shed made out of corrugated tin. Margaret was yelping wildly by the time Charlie opened the door and let in enough light to see Dixie knotted up with rope to the aluminum legs of an old pinball machine, her mouth muffled up with tape.

"Dixie," Charlie screamed. "Dixie! Are you all right?" She ran toward her friend and started to undo the rope and tape, with John Lawless bending over to help, the dogs licking everyone's hands and face.

Once she was unfettered, Dixie jerked the sheriff down to his knees and put her chin square with his, yelling, "Ask him."

Charlie looked at her blankly.

"Ask who?"

"This half-assed, pint-sized can of weasel beans," she muttered, clamoring up to her feet and rubbing her ankles where the rope had burned and scratched against her skin.

"Hold on a minute," Lawless stammered, as his manner grew more hesitant, and his feet were backpedaling to the door.

"I'm talking about you and that home-grown stack of lard Paddy Murphy," she yelled. She realized as she looked at Charlie that her friend was clueless, so she took a deep breath and explained.

"After I took the fax memo up to my room, I realized that I had heard Murphy talk about what a 'great story' was going to come out of the gambling boat's maiden voyage, so I thought I'd find out how much Paddy knew. I took off to find him, but no sooner had I left the house, then I see this nitwit Lawless and Murphy come up the walk, and the two of them grab me like I'm carrying yesterday's winnings from the boat. Murphy starts talking some nonsense about a contract he thinks Spence has hidden in the house, and me being the nosy broad I am, he thinks I've seen it. I tell him I don't know what he's talking about, and the next thing I know, he's got a gun stuck into my ribs and Lawless says, 'You take her to the shed and see if she can remember. I'll go into the Three Sisters and poke around there.'"

Charlie turned to see Lawless pull his gun out and say with a sneer, "All right, everybody stay calm. No need for more dead bodies piling up around this town. Just tell me where Spence kept the contract on the harbor development. There's a bit of forgery on one of the signatures, and I'm doing my law-abiding best to bring the swindler to justice."

"For a small fee, I suppose."

Everyone turned and looked to see Paddy Murphy lunging toward Lawless, helped by his mutt who tore at the Police Chief's ankle, making him drop the gun as he winced in pain.

Dixie quickly seized the gun and raised it with a straight arm right at Lawless.

They were frozen there, all of them, in some kind of tableaux, as if they were waiting or hoping for a stage manager to bark out the next move with a command like "cut" or "house lights down." They heard only the steamboat whistle floating toward them from the river.

"Let him go, Dix" Murphy whispered, taking the gun from her hand. "This mess has gone on long enough."

Suddenly, Mrs. Pillsly appeared from around the corner, holding a manila folder.

"Charlie," she exclaimed, "you'll never guess what I found in the library basement!"

Nancy K. Barry was born in Baltimore, Maryland, but has spent the last fifteen years in Iowa. She now lives in Decorah, where she teaches writing and literature at Luther College. Her essays have appeared in The Des Moines Register, Chicago Tribune, Trapeze, *and* Iowa Woman. *She has been a frequent contributor to the "Iowa Voices" series on WOI, and is currently preparing a collection of essays entitled* Lost Badges: Essays on Finding Home.

14

My Dear Charlotte
by Rekha Basu

Charlie took the folder from Mrs. Pillsly, expecting to find in it some newspaper clippings related to Jonah Barnes. Instead, there was a fat, sealed envelope. "Charlotte," it said.

"I found it on the shelf where I keep my purse and sweater," Mrs. Pillsly was saying. "There was a note attached asking me to give it to you."

Charlie's hands trembled. Only one person had ever called her Charlotte—her estranged husband, whose body had washed up on the banks of the Mississippi yesterday. But what on Earth was a letter from him doing in the library basement?

Suddenly, clutching the envelope, she took off running not knowing where she was headed. Someplace private. Someplace away from these crazy people with their tangled motives and schemes. Someplace safe.

She raced to the Three Sisters, up the stairs, and into a second-floor bathroom, where she locked the door and then sank onto the white marble tile floor by the tub. Her mind was racing. Nothing made sense anymore and almost no one could be trusted.

Ripping open the envelope, she made out what

seemed like a letter attached to some document. She pulled out the first page and began to read. It was typed, single-spaced.

"*My Dear Charlotte,*" it began. "*I'm not sure what I did this morning that angered you so, but whatever it was, forgive me.*"

Charlie bit her lower lip, remembering her little outburst over Ken's mind reading and the way Spence had personalized it. Had it only been yesterday morning? So much had happened since then. That was the last contact she had had with the man she had once been willing to scale Mount Everest for, and the fight had been so trivial, so stupid. Yet that would remain his last memory of her, acting childish and hostile. Didn't he know it was because her feelings for him were still so intense?

A lump welling up in her throat, she read on:

> *But undoubtedly, what I am about to tell you will anger you much more than anything I might have said today. Or perhaps you've already started to suspect something and were telling me in your own way. In any case, this letter is a last resort in case I don't come back. I fear nothing at the Three Sisters will be secure when the authorities come prowling.*
>
> *Please remember as you read these difficult words that I never meant to hurt you. I'd do anything to change the outcome and return to the life we once had. It was simply the best.*

Charlie took a deep breath as the tears began to fall.

■

They had met in Chicago on an airplane bound for New York. He was already occupying seat 6B when she arrived, hauling a framed painting wrapped in brown paper—a gift for the friend she was going to visit—along with her wheel-on suitcase.

"Pardon me, but I think you're in my seat," she had said, struggling with the package.

"Oh, so sorry," he said apologetically, rising half-way and not bothering to check his boarding pass. "I must be, then. Say, you wouldn't by chance prefer a window seat, would you?"

He was ruggedly attractive, dressed in light brown Dockers and a tweedy blazer, with sparkling green eyes and a boyish, dimpled smile. He had a slight British lilt in his voice which she later learned came from his time doing graduate work in London.

"I guess that'd be OK," Charlie said graciously. Why would anyone not want a view of the beautiful Chicago skyline, she wondered as she squeezed past him to claim the window seat. She loved looking down over the city, picking out Wrigley Field and the Sears Tower. It was especially breathtaking framed in the pale pink early evening sky.

Charlie pulled out her *New Yorker* and flipped to the listings in the front, looking for exhibits and off-off Broadway plays to see with Ada. Spence closed his eyes and seemed to be drifting off to sleep. But when the stewardess announced take-off and the propellers began to clamor, she noticed his eyelids were clenched tightly and his fingers were clutching the armrest so hard his knuckles were almost white from the effort.

"Excuse me," she said, giving his sleeve a little tug. "Are you all right?"

"I'm—fine—really," he said, not at all convincingly. "It's just—planes and I don't quite get along."

Charlie grinned. There was something endearing about an otherwise self-possessed man harboring a mortal fear of flying. It gave him a lovable sort of vulnerability.

"You'll be fine," she said reassuringly. "I've been doing this trip for years."

He settled down a bit after they were in the air. Takeoffs and landings were the worst, he explained later, somewhat self-consciously.

He was going to New York for a meeting of legal-aid attorneys. He had just joined a legal services clinic in, of all places, Bella. He would be defending people of modest means, mostly trying to educate them regarding their rights. Lately, too, he'd been working with a growing population of illegal immigrants who had come from the tumultuous Mexican border towns into the calm Iowa anonymity in search of work.

Most of his time these days was also spent fending off overtures from his father's Des Moines law firm. Corporate law wasn't for him, he explained, noting he didn't go to law school to work with a bunch of stiffs motivated only by protecting their assets.

Charlie talked about her parallel dreams of running a bed and breakfast and being a journalist, though at the moment she was working as a cook at a senior citizen home to pay off her college loans.

They talked for most of the flight, and exchanged phone numbers. And she helped talk him through a rather turbulent landing at La Guardia.

It turned out both were staying near the Village, she with her poet friend, Ada, whom she'd gone to college with and went to visit once a year, and he at a modest hotel. The three of them met the next night at The Cookery to hear one of Ada's favorite jazz pianists, Esther Blue—then sat up late by the fountain in Washington Square Park and talked about Iowa and New York, poetry and law, music and muffins.

Ada pronounced him a mensch.

Back in Iowa, Charlie and Spence started spending lots of time together. He'd come by the home where she worked in his beat-up Ford Taurus and amuse the residents with his vast repertoire of stories while waiting for Charlie to get off work. Then they'd go picnicking by the river, or to readings at the Feather Anchor Bookstore, and sometimes take boat rides under moonlit skies. It was love as she had only imagined it, and getting married, when they did, soon after, seemed written in the cards.

But a few years into the marriage, things started to change. Their efforts to have a baby continued to fail, causing regular heartache. Suddenly Spence caved in to the pressures from the family law firm, moving Charlie and himself to Des Moines and going to work among the stiffs he had once derided. Their standard of living rose—they paid off her college loan and bought a beautiful house on Waterbury Road—but Charlie felt the corporate life had fundamentally altered Spence and his values. He seemed to be getting sucked into it in ways she found offensive. Suddenly he was lecturing anyone who would listen about how the needy had to pull themselves up by their bootstraps, and how America wasn't big enough for every wretched refugee who decided to make it home. It became increasingly important to him to make it within a certain social milieu rather than to do meaningful work.

Many of these social functions she'd beg off of, preferring a book with a point to the inane conversation and pretentiousness. Their estrangement grew.

Still, she secretly hoped things might change back when they moved back to Bella and he started his own firm and she opened the Three Sisters. Maybe, she reasoned, the old Spence might resurface. But he only grew more remote. Then a year ago, he dropped the bomb: he wanted out of the marriage.

■

Now he was dead, and here she was, sitting on a cold bathroom floor about to read of some secret life he'd been living. Shuddering, she picked up the letter and continued.

> *There is no easy way to say this, so let me just dive in. For the last few years, I've been living a deceitful life, a life I no longer recognize myself in. It began when I was still at Legal Aid and Paula Swenson came to see me.*
>
> *She was desperate, broke, and in need of a lawyer.*

Although she'd crafted a new identity for herself as a pastor, she was dogged by an unsavory past, and a trade she kept being lured back into. She'd been entrapped by a police officer, busted yet again for prostitution and cocaine. There was something of a scared child buried beneath that hard-talking demeanor. I thought she had the makings of a fighter if she could ever wrest herself free of that pathetic lifestyle. Anyway, her case epitomized much of what I believed I was fighting for—the little person taking on the law-enforcement establishment, a misguided woman seeking love, but used and discarded by the system and every man she'd come in contact with. I guess I saw potential in her, some spunk, some attitude.

I said I'd help her for free. We started spending more time together in the course of preparing her defense, and—well—one night we were working late on her case and one thing just kind of led to another. I didn't mean for it to happen. I was just trying to comfort her. It didn't mean anything.

About a year later, she showed up at my door with a baby. She said it was my child.

Charlotte, because of the problems you and I were having conceiving, I never thought I could father a child and I had told her that. Now there she was, with this infant she claimed was mine, saying it was all my fault! And I guess it was.

She wanted me to divorce you and marry her. Well that was out of the question. I couldn't even tell you about it. I knew how much pain it would cause you, considering our own situation. She threatened to expose me, charge me with breaking the code of my pro-

fession and taking advantage of a helpless client. I could have been disbarred. Everything I'd worked toward would have been lost. Well, I couldn't risk that. I had to buy her silence and it was costly.

As the months wore on, her demands grew greater. If I could just make enough money to get her off my back, then I hoped this mess would go away.

So I finally gave in to my father and joined the firm, thinking maybe I'd make a lot fast and then quit and go back to our old life. I knew you didn't like leaving Bella, or my caving in. I knew we were drifting apart.

But you can't do a job like that and not get caught up in the lifestyle. Making money felt good. You know, Charlotte, idealism doesn't pay the bills.

Anyway, I hoped when we moved back here, you and I would regain our foothold together.

That's when I got involved with a group of people who may ultimately cost me my life. These developers had been trying for a long time to get a license for a floating casino, but as you know, public opinion was dead set against it. Larry Thomas approached me. They were willing to pay well to mute the opposition and get the county's green light. I talked it over with some guys I knew, in particular Paddy Murphy, who was in tight with the local political establishment, and the decision was made to—well—clear a path for the developers. To spell that out for you, Charlotte my dear, that meant bribes had to be given. And they were taken.

Paula, we realized, could be useful to us. She was enlisted to fake religious opposition to the project.

The truth is, all the other opponents had been bought off. But she was slippery. She and Jonah Barnes had another agenda. She kept threatening to expose Thomas, so he had to keep paying her off. And then she also started threatening the people who had their hands out, people like Floyd Delmer.

Now we're all in danger and no one knows who to trust anymore, because anyone who gets caught might sing.

In this envelope is a contract for the harbor development. It's potentially explosive and the authorities may be onto it. Guard it carefully. A lot of people could be harmed if it gets into the wrong hands. By leaving it with you, I realize I've put you at some risk, too. I left the marriage rather than drag you into all this. But it's not safe with me.

If my body suddenly turns up in some ditch, I feel at least you deserve an explanation. We had so much promise, Charlotte. I never lived up to your expectations of me, and I'll never stop regretting that.

Just be careful who you trust. I'll make contact as soon as it's safe.

Yours always,
Spence

Before she could even catch her breath, Charlie heard a pounding on the bathroom door, followed by Ken's voice.

"Charlie" he was saying urgently. "Charlie, open up! We need to talk!"

Rekha Basu moved to Des Moines in 1991 to work at The Des Moines Register, *where she began as an editorial writer and is now a columnist. She has lived in New York, New Delhi, Bangkok, Boston, Woodstock and Albany, New York, and assorted other places. She has been published in* The New York Times, The International Herald Tribune, USA Today, The Miami Herald, The Los Angeles Times, *and* The Nation, *as well as in other media. She says this is her first honest attempt at making a story up.*

15

"Be Careful Who You Trust"

by Eric Woolson

Charlie felt stinging anger.

"Damn you, Spence! How could you be so reckless to get yourself into something so stupid?" she whispered. "Did you think I wouldn't have forgiven your indiscretion? I would have done anything for you. Don't you know we could have found a way, together, to stop Paula's blackmail?"

Ken pounded on the bathroom door again. His voice was more urgent now. "Charlie, open the door now!" he demanded.

"Go away!" she ordered, folding the contract and tucking it into her back pocket. The contract for the harbor development. That damned contract. That's what really stirred her ire. If that was the reason Spence ended up with a bullet in his chest, why did he give it to her? What could he have possibly been thinking? Why, for God's sake, didn't he mail it to his father's law firm or the FBI or DCI or someplace where someone would know what to do with it?

"You don't want me to go away," Ken insisted. "I may be the only person who can keep you from getting killed."

Charlie didn't stop to weigh the gravity of the situation. "I'm safe in here. At least for now. And I want to be alone," she insisted.

"You're not safe," Ken argued. "Not in this town." He took a deep breath. "Listen, I think I've figured out what's going on. Spence's murder— it wasn't a professional hit. Neither were the others. But that's what's so scary. They shouldn't have happened. And that's why I think you're in danger. I don't think your husband was supposed to die yesterday. The killer just panicked. And that's why I believe you're in danger. You have to get out of here."

Charlie thought about yesterday morning. She'd said it herself, Ken was a pretty good journalist. She knew he was a better journalist than she was and probably could ever hope to be. He was certainly a better investigator than Chief Lawless or the Sheriff. Maybe he did have it all figured out.

"Come on!" he urged. "Let's get out of here. Now." It was his final, insistent word that unnerved her. She looked at Spence's letter. *"Just be careful who you trust."* Her head began to spin as she looked at the words. She could practically hear Spence's voice: *"Just be careful who you trust."*

She looked up at the door, knowing Ken was on the other side and growing more anxious by the moment for her to come out.

Why? she wondered. Why is he so desperate to get me out of town? What do I really know about this guy?

"Just be careful who you trust," She heard Spence say softly.

"Charlie. Come out now!" Ken demanded.

Charlie scrambled into the tub, unlocked the window and pushed open the storm window. She clambered onto the roof, hoping he wouldn't hear her escape, only to be waiting for her when she reached the ground. Never one for heights, she nervously crawled over the top of the roof, down the backside to the tree branch that she'd meant to have removed last fall. Each time snow fell during the winter she had cursed herself for not having enough money to have the old maple tree pruned to prevent this branch from crashing through the roof. Now, she was glad the tree was there to provide an escape route. She only hoped she could hold on to the massive trunk long enough to reach the ground safely.

"Charlie!"

Ken's yell made her heart skip a beat. Her left hand lost its hold on the branch, and she dangled precariously thirty feet off the ground for a moment until she valiantly regained her grip.

"Charlie, I know you're out here," Ken hollered. He sounded angry now. She could tell by the sound and direction of his voice that he was calling from the bathroom window.

"He doesn't know where I am," she breathed heavily from a combination of fright and exertion. "Not yet, anyway."

She needed to get out of the tree and reach the safety of the nearby woods.

No one knew much about Mrs. Pillsly's past. The townspeople didn't really consider her secretive. It was just that she always had a knack for turning the conversation away from herself with her questions about others. People just thought she was polite. And, besides, who in Bella didn't enjoy talking about themselves and their own views more than listening to someone else.

Whatever the reason, Mrs. Pillsly's past remained just that: past. Of course, it went without saying that Pillsly wasn't always her last name. That was, after all, a fairly hard and fast rule whenever a woman affixed a "Mrs." in front of her name. Before she'd settled in Bella, Edna Pillsly was Edna Davies. Hers was not exactly a household name, but it was one that was bound to have been recognized by someone who stumbled over her story.

Edna Davies was the first female agent with the Iowa Bureau of Criminal Investigation, back before the name was changed to the Division of Criminal Investigation in the 1970s. She'd planned a career in law enforcement, and Edna Davies accomplished just about everything she'd ever planned in her life. What she hadn't planned was killing someone. A criminal, yes, but also a real, flesh-and-blood person.

It wasn't supposed to happen that way. BCI agents rarely had to draw their weapons. Some went an entire career without firing a shot. But not Edna Davies—no matter what her plans may have been.

The shooting happened when she was on her way home from a murder investigation late one night. The plot was familiar: a drug addict, a cheap handgun, and a convenience store. This time, though, the robber was dead, and Edna Davies' life was altered forever.

The Internal Affairs investigation and a grand jury both ruled the shooting justified. Edna's passion for justice still burned intensely; however, she couldn't clear her mind of the moment and left the Bureau in search of peace in an anonymous, innocuous existence in Bella.

If Spence had known about Edna's past, or if he'd just been thinking clearly, he probably would have given her the contract and written a separate and harmless farewell to Charlie. But he didn't know. No one in Bella knew about Mrs. Pillsly's past life as Edna Davies.

The same could not be said, however, in Des Moines. Mrs. Pillsly's identity was not a secret.

Charlie dropped the last four feet from the tree to the cold, hard ground. The impact knocked her off her feet, but she bounced up and ran for the nearby woods. Even over her labored breathing she heard footsteps behind her. Someone was chasing her, but she dared not look. She couldn't believe Ken could have caught up with her, and knew in her heart he had not. Now, for a faint moment, she wished he was following her, wished she had let him take her away from Bella.

"God, just let me get to the woods," she prayed. Driven more by exhaustion than reason, Charlie dove into the underbrush as she reached the edge of the woods. She knew she could not remain there for long without being found.

"Charlie," Ken called out from the inn's yard. He was walking, but he was walking in her direction.

He was a pretty good journalist, she thought again. But who had been chasing her, and where was that person now?

She turned away from Ken. Lifting herself from the ground, she was startled when a man clamped his hand over her mouth and pulled her to her feet.

"Sssshhhhh," he advised softly. "Let's get out of here before he finds us. Follow me. My car is parked near Paddy Murphy's house."

Charlie's heart pounded. Ken had scared her half to death and Barry Bullyard had damn near finished her off. But she felt safe with him, and knew he could be trusted.

She heard a thud in front of her as Bullyard tripped over a branch, stump, or some other obstacle in the waning light.

"Damn," he moaned, "I hope I can 'expense out' these pants. I think I just tore the knee."

She was surprised to hear herself laugh, but his complaint was so trivial that it broke the tension. Yes, she thought, she could definitely trust Barry Bullyard.

Ken's ire increased as he stopped, listened, and heard nothing but the low roar and splashing wake of a passing tow and barge. He kicked the ground.

"Damn it," he muttered. "She couldn't have gone far. I've got to find her before they do."

He ran to his car, wondering which direction he should search first.

Charlie slumped in the front seat of Barry Bullyard's black Mitsubishi GT4000.

"Nice car," she said, still catching her breath. "I didn't think reporters made enough to afford this kind of ride."

"They don't," Bullyard replied, turning the key in the ignition to bring the sports car to life. "My boyfriend is an attorney. He's loaded."

Charlie shrugged. "Maybe he'll pay to fix your pants."

Bullyard glared at her. "Whatever."

Charlie suppressed a small smile. Yes, she thought again, she could definitely trust Barry Bullyard. He shoved the stick into first gear and floored the accelerator.

"We've got to get out of here."

For the first time since Ken pounded on the bathroom door, Charlie thought about Dixie.

"We have to go back. We have to find my friend."

"No way," Bullyard said. "I only came to get you because Wild Bill ordered me to. Seems he has a soft spot in his heart for you. But he didn't say anything about friends, relatives, or pets. He told me to get you and get out of Dodge City. And that's exactly what we're going to do."

Bullyard shifted through the gears like a professional race car driver, pushing the GT4000 up to 105 mph on the winding, two-lane highway outside of Bella. He loved to open it up, and this occasion was a perfect excuse to tear up the road.

Charlie knew enough about Bullyard to know that he never took direction. She couldn't figure out why he'd pick today to start.

"Since when did you start following the orders of the city desk?" she asked.

"Since every other person in town started turning up dead," he fired back. "I may be insubordinate, but I'm also a coward. There's no way I'm staying in Bella until they've got a suspect in custody. And with the level of expertise and intelligence that pinhead police chief has, Bella could look like Jonestown before the sun comes up tomorrow."

Charlie had had enough of the witty repartee. "Look, my husband is dead. My house has been ransacked. I don't know where my best friend is. Two other people I know have been murdered. Tell me something that's going to help me."

"I wish I could," Bullyard said, now somber. "I wish I could."

"Where are we going?"

"It's too late to drive back to Des Moines. I figure we'd be safe in Davenport."

Charlie nodded.

"Sounds like a plan. Just slow down, please. I don't want to get killed. Besides, if you don't want to call attention to yourself, you shouldn't be driving at Mach 1."

She has a point, Bullyard thought, easing off the accelerator and glancing up at the rear-view mirror. Now it was his turn to ask the questions.

"Why do you think someone killed your husband?"

Charlie leaned forward and silently retrieved the folded contract from her back pocket. "I don't know. But I'm sure it has something to do with this," she said. "It's the contract for the harbor development."

"What was your husband's role in the deal? Was

he an investor or did he just draw up the documents?"

"I don't know," Charlie lamented, shaking her head. "He didn't tell me much about his work when we were married, and I think we were already separated when he was working on this thing."

"He had to be pretty deeply involved, don't you think? I mean, they wouldn't just kill him for drawing up a few legal papers, would they?" Bullyard fished.

Charlie was becoming exasperated by Bullyard's questions and her lack of answers.

"I don't know, I don't know, I don't know. All right?"

He backed off. "Sorry. I was just trying . . ."

"I know," she apologized. "You were just trying to help."

"Yeah," he nodded.

She took a deep breath. "Ken said . . ."

"Ken who?"

"Ken. Ken, the TV reporter from Japan, Ken," she fumbled. "Ken Wakabayashi."

"Go on."

"Ken said he thinks he knows who killed Spence and the others. He said it was an amateur job, a panic thing."

"How's he know that?" Bullyard pressed.

She felt like a broken record.

"I don't know. He probably would've given me some details but I ran away. That's when you found me."

"You mean, the guy in the backyard was a reporter?" Charlie nodded.

"Yeah. At least I think so. I don't know who or what to believe any more."

"Glad I got to you first. I'd really be in trouble if I let another reporter get you," Bullyard deadpanned.

Charlie remained serious.

"I think we have enough trouble as it is. I just can't figure it out. Spence said the contract was potentially explosive and the authorities may be on to it. I don't know why he wouldn't have gone to them and just turned over the contract."

"Maybe they're involved," Bullyard theorized.

"John Lawless may be involved," she told him. "But Spence could've trusted someone, somewhere. The FBI in Chicago."

"It says a lot that he trusted you," Bullyard said, trying to console her.

"Yeah, it does," she whispered, tears welling in her eyes at the memory of Spence. She opened the glove compartment in a fruitless search for a Kleenex. Neither of them said anything for some time as the early spring scenery swept past and Bullyard continued to eye the rear-view mirror. Finally, he broke the silence.

"Uh, you're going to think I'm paranoid, but I think we're being followed."

Eric Woolson has been Governor Terry Branstad's communications director and press secretary since January 1996.

Prior to that time, Woolson was an award-winning reporter and commentator. He began his journalism career in 1976 as a staff reporter at the Boone News-Republican *at age 17 and later worked as a reporter for the* Madrid Register-News, Guthrie Center Times *and* Guthrian *and* Daily Freeman-Journal *in Webster City. He was the managing editor of the* Daily Gate City *in Keokuk from 1981-83 before becoming a reporter for United Press International in Des Moines.*

Except for a brief stint when he served as a press secretary on the presidential campaign and official staff of U.S. Senator Joseph Biden, Woolson was employed at the Waterloo Courier *from 1984 to 1996, first as its political and legislative writer, and then as the newspaper's editorial page editor.*

Woolson, 40, is a former guest commentator on KUNI Public Radio in Cedar Falls and former panelist on the Iowa Public Television program, Iowa Press. *He is also the author of the book,* Grassley: The Senator from Iowa, *and is a member of The Society of Midland Authors. He and his wife, Debora Blume, have one son, Brooks. They reside in West Des Moines.*

16

Death by the Billboard

by Kate Myers Hanson

A soft drizzle had begun, the intermittent wipers only smearing a milky residue on the windshield. Charlie lowered the passenger window, the smell like geraniums, fresh and earthy. She and Spence often took walks in rain like this. Instead of being angry about his deception, only these small moments when they were so close, when they were at their best together, kept flooding back.

"I think we still have company," Barry Bullyard told her. "Don't turn around and look. We don't want to tip off the driver of that car."

"But who could be following us?

"Hell if I know, but Ken seemed pretty anxious to link up with you back there."

"Link up with me. . ."

Charlie believed at the time that her life had been in danger, but maybe he was just an aggressive reporter. God knows people like that have caused the deaths of celebrities they've covered. But Charlie couldn't figure out why she was such an overnight sensation in Bella.

When Barry slowed down, a clunky green sedan, a Buick or Pontiac from what Charlie could see in the side mirror, slowed down behind them. If Barry turned on his signal to exit off of Highway 52, the car would do the same. Somehow Charlie wasn't frightened by the car. Maybe because it was old, maybe because she was more nervous by having ac-

164   cepted Barry's suggestion to hightail it out of Bella. She could feel the contract in the back pocket of her jeans. Nobody was going to look over that piece of paper before she had a chance to really study it.

Barry shook his head, then smoothed a few strands, blonde mixed with grey, over home plate.

"You've got an interesting town, Charlie. More nuts than a fruitcake." He picked at the tear on his trousers. "I paid three hundred bucks for these—Armani."

"I guess you shouldn't have been traipsing around in the woods after me."

"Damsels in distress are one of my specialties."

"I'll just bet they are."

He winked at her.

"Gents, too."

Charlie had never seen such poor taste in expensive clothes. His green golf shirt, patterned in diamonds, was stretched to its limit over his considerable belly, paired up with blue pants, probably silk and wool. Having money didn't mean you had class. Spence's idea of success it seemed was having his pockets lined with gold.

"Why are you so interested in helping me?" Charlie asked.

"Well, first off, you're a fellow journalist." Charlie snickered.

"Right . . . and Bill Watson sent you up here."

"The thing is, two plus two ain't adding up to four. When Bill ordered me to get my ass in gear, I thought, what the hell, I'll poke around and see what I come up with, maybe learn some more about the casino deal, the money trail . . ."

As they passed an exit sign for the Turkey River Mounds, Charlie could still see the green sedan hanging back like a shadow.

"Get off here, see if that car follows us."

"I'd prefer to be killed in Davenport, not at a Texaco Food Mart in Nowhere'sville."

"Do it," Charlie said. "You don't have to stop. Just get back on the highway after you exit."

"No snacks?"

"Not this time."

Charlie was beginning to feel more comfortable with Bullyard. His humor was refreshing. But she remembered Spence during their first airplane flight together, his panic, the way he pointed out that before each crash there were always unsuspecting passengers laughing. He thought everyone should be solemn during takeoff, deep in prayer. He had told her in his letter, *Be careful who you trust*. She knew Barry was a seasoned reporter and wasn't "saving" her solely because he was a decent man.

"So why have you become my guardian angel?"

Barry pulled off Highway 52, but the green sedan plodded on by, didn't follow them. Charlie turned to get a better look.

"If I didn't know better, I'd say that was Edna Pillsly."

166

"The librarian?"

"Why in the world would she be following us?"

"She's the broad who gave you Spence's letter and the contract. Don't you think it's a little odd she found it in the library? If Spence left it there, it could have been years before she discovered it. Was it sitting out in the open, beside a card catalogue, the petty cash?"

"She told me she found it on a shelf."

"A lot of weird shit going on here, Charlie."

"Oh, I'm probably wrong. It just looked like Edna."

Barry didn't respond but pulled back on the highway. The green sedan had disappeared.

"You never answered me. Why have you taken such an interest in me?"

"You're the key, Charlie . . . to this whole mess."

"Yeah right, I'm in deep with the mob. A regular mafia princess."

Barry glared at her. "Unfortunately, that's probably true. Of course, not of your own doing."

"What're you talking about?"

"Think about it. The fewer people who have an interest in the land deal and casino operations, the bigger the piece of pie will be for those who are left."

"Sounds like you know more than I do."

What Charlie understood was that the husband she had loved was dead, and maybe Paula Swenson was involved in his death, money-grubber that she was. Who else was left? John Lawless and Paddy Murphy weren't smart enough together to rob a 7-Eleven.

"Strings are being pulled outside Bella," said Barry.

"Bill Watson and I did some investigating a while back. The whole deal was ripe for mob activity. A couple numbchucks from South Jersey who had locked up the garbage industry down there got a graduation present. They done good so Papa Martelli set them up in the laundry business in Des Moines."

"Laundry business?"

"Money was being laundered through your father-in-law's upscale law firm in Des Moines. All very smooth. Want to know where that money ended up?"

"I can guess. I never understood how just La Bella Corporation was able to back the land and casino deal. The only principal investors I knew of were Larry Thomas and Jonah and Paula."

"Small potatoes, even with Spence. A Fed informant recently told us that after Spence mortgaged Three Sisters to the hilt, he made you a partner, even put your name on the land contract. He was in it up to his coconuts."

"Nice of you to finally tell me. So you think some hit man killed Spence and the others?"

"Actually I think there are two killers, but neither of them is a professional. Too sloppy."

Charlie's stomach ached, from hunger and from fear. She rolled down the window some more, thinking she might get sick. Sloppy . . . Spence's face was twisted in an awful expression, eyebrows raised as if in surprise. Since his death, for just a few seconds she felt peaceful—until she remembered. It was the remembering that would take her breath away.

"Barry," she said. "I want to go back to Bella."

"But we're over halfway to Davenport. I have

friends in the Bureau there. They could protect you."

"I don't care. Dixie is back there and doesn't have any protection. No telling what could happen."

"Watson'll have my ass."

Barry drove another quarter of a mile and then turned around on a gravel farm road, his tires spitting out gray plumes of dust. A sign on the telephone pole read, "Baby chicks for sale."

Edna Pillsly, a.k.a. Edna Davies, watched from a bridge overpass until she saw the car Charlie was riding in, a black sportscar, turn around and head back north, toward Bella she presumed. Why had Charlie even left with Bullyard in the first place? Edna had no reason to believe he would harm Charlie, but she wasn't taking any chances. She found it comforting that accessing information from law enforcement was still easy. All it took was money. With Pastor Paula temporarily out of the picture, the only loose cannon was Spence's father, Gerald Wood, who had big ties to organized crime. His law firm often represented major crime bosses in Chicago, New York, and New Jersey.

Wood had agreed to help Spence out of his financial difficulties with Paula in return for a piece of the land deal and casino. This made Lawrence Thomas and Jonah Barnes nervous. Paula also didn't want anybody to have a bigger slice than she had, and she certainly didn't want Charlie and Spence linked together in this deal. When the fat man smokes a cigar, the fat lady exhales. Charlie could talk. With her name on that contract, Edna knew Charlie was in danger. She would inherit his rights for future income from *La Bella,* and would own Three Sisters free and clear. Wood had paid off the mortgage as part of the deal with his son. Maybe this was the only time in Charlie's life that Edna could protect her. That was the least a mother could do.

At the age of sixteen, she had given Charlie to the Simons in a private adoption her parents had arranged, all of them living in Oak Park, a suburb of Chicago. The Simons were both teachers, childless after ten years of marriage. In high school, Mrs. Simons had taught Edna "World Literature" in her junior year. There was a kindness and gentility about Mrs. Simons that Edna even tried to imitate as a librarian. Charlie must have been a lucky charm, for the Simons had two daughters of their own in the next two years whom they named Emily and Anne.

When Jane Simons died, Charlie was in college, and it became more difficult to keep tabs on her. Charlie's move to Bella seemed providential to Edna. Time and chance, and now mother and daughter would finally be together as a family. But then there was Spence, a selfish womanizer who had many of his father's weaknesses for shady money deals. Spence had put Charlie in great danger.

The afternoon Spence died, Edna walked down to the harbor as she did most afternoons. Her constitutional, she called it—a short power walk—which was always invigorating since she seldom got out of the library or even took a lunch hour. She saw Spence and Paula arguing near the landing but far from the gathering casino crowd. They backed away into a grove of trees, partially obscured by a billboard for *La Bella Riverboat* and Casino. Paula gesticulated wildly with her hands, the movement like the flapping of wings as if she were a bird trying to escape.

Edna moved closer to hear them, kneeling next to a hedgerow of redbuds. Paula was trying to squeeze more money out of Spence to buy her silence. She was ready to expose him—his philandering, the baby, the money deals, the mortgage on Three Sisters. But Spence waved her off.

"You go right ahead and do whatever you want," he said, displaying an arrogance that made Edna furious. How could he have cared so little about Charlie's feelings?

Paula tried to slap Spence across the face, but he grabbed her slender arm in mid-air and threw her to the ground.

"You'll pay, Spence. . . . You sure as hell will pay." She climbed the embankment, walking so close to Edna that Edna could have reached out and touched the hem of her gabardine skirt. She turned one more time.

"Just remember, Spence. Nobody messes with Associated Casino Enterprise. Nobody. They'll take care of your precious Charlie, too."

Edna had always known she could kill again, not as an officer of the law, but as a mother protecting her child. She literally watched herself from a distance, a tall matronly woman who strode toward Spence holding a small caliber handgun in the pocket of her navy blue blazer, a tiny champagne rose pinned on the lapel. Noise from the boat rose and fell in

waves, music wafted from the main deck and passengers cheered as the boat prepared to leave the
dock. Firecrackers popped, set off by children on
shore. High school students dressed in silky red
shirts and white trousers stood at attention waiting
for a signal from Mr. Barber, the band leader—his
arms raised, baton high. When his arms dropped,
they played energetically.

A Sousa march, Edna thought as she moved closer
to Spence, down the embankment. She took a moment to straighten her skirt, to brush off the dirt.
Spence smiled, as if amused, and actually walked
toward Edna at this moment. Facing him, she fired
once into his stomach. He fell beside the billboard,
curled up like a homeless man Edna often saw in town.

Edna leaned over Spence and searched him, a pro-
cedure she had not forgotten from her law enforcement days. A letter to Charlie in the right pocket of
his jacket. Apparently his intention to give it to
Charlie had caused him to be so bold with Paula.
The letter was confessional and weak, and inside was
the contract with Charlie's name forged. She would
give all of this to Charlie when the time was right.

The inside pocket of his jacket contained an envelope filled with hundred-dollar bills, as much as
twenty thousand, Edna thought. Of course, she put
it back but wondered to whom Spence intended to
give the money. Obviously he was planning to meet
someone soon.

Edna looked around to make sure she hadn't been
observed. Smoke still lingered in the air from the
bonfire before the maiden voyage. She left in the gray

light and confusion. Looking back she could see someone else sliding down the last few feet of the embankment on his or her derriere. This person carried something in one hand. A shoe box? No, smaller.

Edna scurried away.

Kate Myers Hanson (Katie) received her M.F.A. from the University of Iowa Writers' Workshop in 1998. Eventually, she would like to live in Iowa permanently.

Currently, she is the Visiting Professor and Writer at Northern Michigan University in Marquette, where she teaches fiction and is Editor of Northern Passages, *their literary review. Katie's short fiction has been widely published, appearing in* The North American Review, Shenandoah, South Carolina Review, Prairie Schooner, *and other publications. She has recently completed a collection of stories,* Book of Names, *and is hard at work on a novel. Katie has two wonderful children, Louise and Tommy.*

17

Time and Chance

by Carolyn Lieberg

Barry drove slowly down Bella's Main Street. He'd argued with Charlie most of the way back, dreading this return and what it might mean. Charlie couldn't imagine that someone would want *her* dead.

"I can't leave Dixie stranded," Charlie said for maybe the fifth time.

"I know. I know." Barry was a bit exasperated. "Let's try Joe's Bar and Grille before we venture back to the Bates Motel."

"Barry! That's my Bed and Breakfast you're im-pugning—" A sudden turn into the only parking spot on the street pressed Charlie against the door.

Barry flipped the headlights off.

"Stay here. I think it's safer. I'll be right back." He offered to leave the keys. "Do you want to listen to the radio?" It was Al Shares and Bob Dorr.

"Hmm, no thanks. I think I'll just listen to Bella." Charlie rolled down her window.

"I'll look for Lawless and Schmidt, too. We need to find out what's going on." Barry slipped out of the car and closed the door firmly.

The familiar noise and bustle of Bella made Charlie feel fairly safe. Shouts and laughter, people calling back and forth—it was as if the murders hadn't happened.

Charlie reached around and pulled the contract out of her pocket. Somehow, she thought, the piece of paper wasn't safe enough there. She began unbuttoning her blouse and then looked down at her shoes. She could barely see them, and, struck by a thought, she suddenly reached down and slid the folded sheet under the floor mat.

"Yeah," she said to herself, "that's better." She stretched back again and was taking a deep breath when her car door jerked open and a firm hand yanked her up.

"Bar—" she started, then got a look at who had actually grabbed her. "Ken!"

She grasped at the car door, but it was too late. She was off balance and Ken pulled her hard. She stumbled the few feet to the open door of his car.

"Ken! Don't! Let go! Help!" she shouted, but no one on the street seemed to notice. She kept struggling against him until she saw Dixie in the back seat— bound and gagged.

Charlie jumped in and crawled into the back seat. She began fumbling with the twine holding Dixie's wrists. Ken slid in and took off.

"Get in the front seat, Charlie!" he yelled.

"No way, you maniac!"

He drove like a madman, weaving between cars and pedestrians, a flood of yells and honking followed their trail down Main Street.

"You'd better leave Miss Dixie alone," Ken warned in a menacing voice as he tried to keep the car on the road. "You have no idea the trouble you're in, Charlie."

Headlights appeared in their lane and Ken jumped the curb to keep from hitting the truck coming at them. The women slammed to one side of the car and then back to the other.

"Criminy, Ken, you're going to get us killed—probably just what you want!" Charlie eased the gag off Dixie's mouth.

Dixie spoke in a low voice. "You can't listen to this guy, Charlie. He's really lost it. I've got to get out of here."

"Damn!" Ken snapped. "Who's on our tail?" Charlie whirled around, "Oh lord, I hope it's Barry!" At this speed, they'd be at the Three Sisters in a couple of minutes.

"Barry?" Dixie said, holding her wrists up to remind Charlie that she still wasn't free.

"He saved me from Ken," Charlie whispered as loud as she had to. "Ken was chasing me into the woods. Barry and I drove south, but I couldn't stand leaving you here." Charlie got one knot undone and started on the second one. She glowered at the back of Ken's head.

"Slow down, you lout!" she shouted at him. They drove under a streetlight, and so did the car behind them.

"Was that a Lincoln? Who owns a Lincoln?" Ken asked. "What in the hell is that doing here? What does Paddy Murphy drive?"

"I don't know," said Charlie.

"WHAT DOES PADDY MURPHY DRIVE?"

Ken swerved harder, as if that would help the car disappear. "Hell, there's more than one car after us. Dixie," Ken shouted, "surely you know what the prez drives. Your hands are in this up to your neck."

The Three Sisters was approaching on their right. Ken drove right into the parking area, through it, and headed over the long lawn that led down to the Mississippi.

"What are you doing?" shouted Charlie.

"Saving your life," Ken shouted back. He killed the lights and sped on while the women shouted at him. He suddenly veered to the right.

"Look!" Charlie pointed to the gambling boat and the reflection of lights on the water. The car was aimed south, but the wet grass ignored the lay of the wheels. Instead of heading toward Davenport, the car was still heading toward Illinois. It skidded toward the water and the two women fell against each other as the slope dipped down to the river. The car twisted slightly on its way to a small curve in the shoreline where a strip of mud was the last stop before a drop-off into the river. The left side of the car suddenly found traction in the goo and the momentum pushed the car up on its left two wheels where it teetered between Iowa and the chilly waters of the Mississippi.

"Don't move."

"Roll down the windows!"

"Keep the windows up."

"Get out."

"Don't move!"

Everyone had a solution.

Meanwhile the chasing cars—now four in number—pulled up by the shoreline and stopped. Their headlights illuminated the strange scene of the car balancing on the edge of disaster. Gamblers on the deck of *La Bella* were drawn to the sight. A small silence seemed to fall among some of them as the teetering car captured their attention. The pulsing light on the sheriff's car mirrored the urgency everyone was feeling.

Barry began running toward the car. Sheriff Schmidt pulled on the end of the winch attached to his front bumper, and Doris and Mary Lou slid out of the sheriff's back seat.

"We've got to keep it from tipping in, or they'll all be goners!" he yelled, as he waved the hook.

Edna climbed out of her car and walked as fast as she could to the commotion.

More people from the casino drifted outside to see the show on the shore. "What's happening, Edna?" asked Mary Lou as the librarian stood beside her.

Edna whirled to face the woman and a quick smile of recognition flashed across her face. "Long time, Mary Lou. A long time."

"I wondered if I'd run into you."

"Isn't this awful." Edna turned back to the shore, too distracted by the unsteady car to talk further. She watched Sheriff Schmidt throw the end of the winch over to the car once. Nothing caught and he pulled it back.

Edna stepped up to him and grabbed it out of his hand. "Excuse me Sheriff. I used to be good at this."

"It's true, Sheriff. Trust me," said Mary Lou.

"Huh?!" the sheriff said. "What is this? The Ladies Aid of Iowa to the rescue?"

"Watch your mouth, Mr. Schmidt," Doris warned. "You're darn lucky to be getting some talent here."

178

Edna made a loop with the rope as if it were a lasso, swung it around her head a few times (the others ducked), and let loose. Metal hit glass and scraped along and then stopped. The hook had caught on something. It wouldn't matter what as long as it held.

Sheriff Schmidt ran back to his car and turned on the winch. It slowly began winding, drew taut, and his car slid on the slick grass as the winch caught the weight. Suddenly the wayward car flopped back down on all four wheels, though it was still on a steep angle toward the river.

The audience on *La Bella* burst into cheers and applause and began drifting away from the deck rail.

The car doors opened and Ken tumbled out of the front. Charlie and Dixie fell out of the back. Barry put his arm around Charlie and led her away to the Three Sisters. Edna followed. The sheriff, Doris, and Mary Lou helped Ken and Dixie, who both seemed unsteady, over the slick grass and into the Victorian house.

"Do you have whiskey in this B & B?" Barry asked Charlie.

She shook her head. "But you'll find lots of herbal tea. The basket's next to the stove." She flopped down in an overstuffed chair.

In a minute, Barry returned to the living room with a tray of mugs and tea bags. "I put some water on to heat. Remind me, though, OK?"

Ken was pacing. The sheriff had his hand on his gun, though he hadn't taken it out of his holster. Edna perched on one arm of the chair Charlie had collapsed into and patted her shoulder absentmind-edly. Dixie leaned against the other arm, fussing with one of her fingernails and looking into the dark hall-way that led up the stairs. Doris and Mary Lou were across the room hovering over the television stand and fiddling with the buttons on the VCR.

"I want some answers, folks," Sheriff Schmidt said.

"Answers!" Charlie spit out. "The victims aren't even in their graves yet. Can't we have a little peace?" Her voice echoed in the still room, and she threw her head back and sighed. "Sorry for the outburst, Sheriff. I don't know if I'm coming or going."

"Well, actually," said Barry "we don't know who's coming, but we know who's gone, and we'd like to keep you from going, too, Charlie."

He threw a nasty look at Ken again.

Ken raised his hands in a motion that landed some-where between prayer and helplessness. "Look, Barry," he started. "You seem to have some—"

Suddenly Police Chief John Lawless barged in, tugging on a bedraggled woman in black, red, fringe, net, and satin that covered the basic parts but not much else.

Mary Lou looked her up and down. "She's back," she said and returned to the VCR, sliding a tape in with a clean electronic click.

Edna said under her breath, "Pastor Paula."

Chief Lawless looked at the sheriff. "So I brought

this one in, and I called Paddy over. What now?"

Charlie glanced up from her chair.

Suddenly the video came on with loud static and a gray screen.

"Listen, everybody," said Ken. "My high-end mike really does a job." The VCR was playing a tape of yesterday morning's fog, which revealed nothing. Then the scream of a hawk startled everyone, but it ended and there was only a clicking sound that sliced into the useless picture.

"Impressive mike," the police chief said, "but not much else."

"Is that some insect?" Doris said.

The sheriff shrugged his shoulders and looked at Ken, who wore a knowing expression. They looked at the screen again, which continued to show nothing but fog.

The nature sounds were suddenly drowned by Jonah's voice. "No! What are you doing? Are you nuts? Here, look, wait! Look, I'll burn it. See? I won't show it to anybody."

There was a short silence, a little more clicking, and then the sound of a lighter igniting. "See? There it goes. Nobody will know. I won't tell a soul. Your secret will go to hell with me, I promise."

Another silence fell across the gray screen. No one spoke on the film or in the room. The crackling of the paper burning dwindled away, and the odd clicking started again.

"NO!" Jonah shouted. "ACE will take care of—" There was a shot and a soft thud and swift footsteps through the grass. The video ended, and the screen went blue. Paula put her hands over her face.

"Oh, Jonah," she moaned softly.

"As if you didn't know," said Chief Lawless, with disgust dripping from his voice.

"Where did that video come from?" Charlie asked.

"We found Ken looking at it this afternoon," Doris said.

"I'm so sorry you ladies got dragged into this." Charlie leaned toward Doris and Mary Lou apologetically, remembering her role as an innkeeper. "Oh," she stood up quickly, "the water!"

"I'll get it," Barry said, brushing past her.

"Don't worry about it, Charlie. About us, I mean," said Mary Lou. "I'm from the Gaming Commission, here to see what was up with *La Bella*."

"Gaming Commission?"

"I'm not Doris," Doris said. "My name is really Carmen Mooney."

"Carmen!" Charlie's mouth dropped.

Doris looked at the others. "Charlie and I never met, but I knew she'd recognize my name. I used to work for Spence's dad, until I figured out that their accounts were strange. I heard enough talk around the firm to know that this land deal was as crooked as the old Mississippi itself. Chicago money, forged signatures, stacked gaming tables—it was bad, bad, bad. I got out before anyone suspected me of knowing a thing and went straight to work undercover. I wasn't going to have that filthy big-city gambling disease contaminate Iowa."

Doris, or Carmen, straightened her battery-operated sweatshirt with its flashing Queen of Hearts crown. "This is a camera, by the way. Not as good as your mike, Ken, but pretty clever, eh? James Bond would have loved it. And Edna, you would have, too, in your days with the BCI. Anyway, we expected to gather some evidence this weekend, but we had no idea bodies would be falling left and right."

"Edna?" several people asked at once, looking at their librarian. She shrugged her shoulders and smiled at them.

Barry carried in a tray with mugs, tea bags, and hot water. He gave Edna a big smile. "Jig's up?" he said, as he put the tray on the coffee table. Charlie helped Barry hand the mugs around.

"Nothing else can surprise me," Charlie said, sitting back in her chair wearily.

Paula sighed. "Get on with it, boys. Let's get this over with."

Ken darted over to Mary Lou and snatched the videotape. "I need this for my documentary. My bosses have been pressuring me for a sensational story, but I didn't expect to actually find one."

"Not so fast, son, not so fast," Sheriff Schmidt said. "We'll need it as evidence."

"I'll make you a copy."

Everyone seemed to be waiting for the next question to be answered.

"The tape doesn't do much for us, though, does it?" Lawless said, taking a sip of the hot drink. "You can't see anything."

The silence of the room was broken by a tapping, a clicking, a ticking, and all eyes turned to Dixie, whose fingernail was tick-tick-ticking away on her mug.

"Yeah, there's only one voice," Dixie said frantically as she slid her fingers firmly around her mug. "Only Jonah's voice is on that tape."

"Yeah," said the sheriff. "Why is that, Dixie? Why didn't you say something to the poor fella when you were about to snuff him?"

"What?"

"Come on, Dixie. Those were your fingernails on that tape—probably clicking on the side of the gun."

"But I was at Joe's Bar and Grille, having a drink."

"No, you weren't," Ken said. "You showed up there, ordered a whiskey, had one big swallow, and then left in time to walk down the street with Charlie, sounding a little drunk, from what one witness reported."

Everyone looked back at the hairdresser. Dixie looked from Charlie to Ken to the Sheriff. She dropped her mug and collapsed to the floor in tears, "I couldn't do it. I couldn't kill Charlie," she sobbed. "They wanted her next!"

"ME?!?" Charlie yelled. She squatted next to Dixie. "Dixie, what are you saying?" She put her hands on Dixie's shoulders which shook with sobs. "Of course you couldn't kill me, Dixie. I'm your friend."

"Charlie," she said through her broken voice, "I killed Jonah and then Larry Thomas, and I was supposed to kill you. Paddy—Paddy isn't just Paddy. He's Dwayne's brother."

"Of the D's—Delbert, Dwayne, Darryl and Dewey?" Charlie asked quietly.

Dixie nodded, and wiped her hands on her jeans. "I'm glad it's over. Dwayne and Paddy are mixed up with that Chicago money Doris told you about. They just kept pushing me."

"What about Paula?" Charlie asked.

"Yeah, I was involved—spying for the bastards and trying to make money besides. I watched you, Dixie. Then I couldn't stand it any more. I'm tired of all the lies. Spence wasn't the father of my child. I only told him that so he'd marry me. Then when Jonah was killed, I decided to split."

"What's Ken doing in all of this?" Charlie asked. Dixie tightened her fist briefly and looked at her. "Nothing—although they were ready to pull anyone in who'd come, I think. All of 'em expecting a piece of that fat cigar, right Ken? No one expected the fat lady to exhale though. Ha! Well, I'm exhaling all right. I'm exhaling so much, I'm singing."

"Why could they—" Charlie began.

The door opened again, and all eyes turned to Paddy.

"Hey, what's the reunion going on here? Lawless? Sheriff?" He nodded his head around as if he was up to his usual glad-handing. "The boat's growing money like a regular tree. Let's pop the cork on some champagne!"

"It's over, Paddy," Dixie said, standing up and planting her feet angrily on the floor.

"What? What?!" Paddy spat it out as if he didn't want to know the answer.

"I don't care any more. Things can't get any worse. You and your Chicago scum. I'm not scared any more."

"But folks . . . " he began.

"We figured it out," Ken said, with a bit of pride in his voice.

"The kidnapping?" Paddy asked. "How could you—how did you find out about that?"

"Kidnapping? We were talking about fingernails, I believe," Sheriff Schmidt said with a forceful voice.

Paddy wafted a smug smile around the room. "So you didn't quite figure everything out." He took a step toward Dixie and grabbed her shirt as though she were a piece of wet laundry.

She shoved him back as Charlie lurched at him.

"Let go of her, you creep."

Paddy backed off.

The room was dead silent.

"This little lady was involved in a kidnapping a couple of husbands ago," he said.

Dixie hung her head but spit anger through her teeth. "It was so long ago, Paddy."

"Yeah, it was. She was married to my brother, Dwayne, and the two wanted a baby more than anything. One day she spotted a wee one strapped into a car seat in the middle of a K-Mart parking lot and just decided that little girl must be the day's blue-light special."

"I knew it was wrong. I gave her back!" Dixie shouted bitterly.

"Yeah, two weeks later," Paddy said. "Doesn't count with the law. Kidnapping is kidnapping. But you see they never caught her. After Dwayne there was Darryl, and the move here to Bella was just the safest place to be. You didn't realize old Paddy was even here for a while, did you, Dixie? Yeah, she and

Dwayne weren't real family-oriented—except for the one they couldn't make. Dixie was mighty surprised the day I introduced myself to her. And even more surprised to learn that I had her past in my pocket. We always figured a long stretch in prison, maybe life."

"I've got that anyway, now" Dixie said quietly. The sheriff chimed in. "You did his dirty work so he wouldn't tell the world about yours?"

"And then you ended up with everyone's crime on your head," said Edna sadly.

Charlie put her arms around her friend. "I'm so sorry, Dixie."

Dixie pulled herself free to face Paddy. "And you used it, you scumbag, to get me to do your bidding. You thug! It was Threaten Jonah! Scare Jonah! Get Jonah to sell out! And when none of that worked, it was Kill Jonah!"

Paddy's jaw dropped, but he brought it up quickly. "You think you can blame me?"

She buried her face in her hands again, but her muffled words fell out clearly. "You sent him a letter telling him about me. He waved it in my face and he threatened to tell Charlie unless I found the contract." Dixie pulled her hands slowly to her sides. "You scum! You blackmailed me into doing exactly what you wanted. One by one, you swore you'd kill every casino owner until you were left with that big sweet pot all to yourself. No inheritance rights, you smart boys wrote into the document. What a recipe for murder."

"Where is that contract?" Edna asked. Everyone ignored her.

"But Jonah burned the letter from Paddy, didn't

he?" Ken asked in a matter of fact tone. He seemed to have known everything for hours.

"You think that would have kept him from leaning on me for something else? I would have had Paddy and Jonah and the rest of those swine extorting the life out of me."

"I think they did," Mary Lou said.

"And Spence?" Doris asked. "No one's said anything about him."

Edna began to speak, "Aaah, I—"

"No you didn't." Dixie spoke up.

Edna folded her hands together and looked hard at Dixie.

"He wasn't dead, only wounded," Dixie explained. "I finished him off by tying that brick on and dumping him in the river."

Dixie looked at Charlie and dropped her head. Edna sighed in relief.

"So where is the contract?" Barry asked.

"It's in your car, under the floor mat," Charlie said. Barry left the room.

"With the Three Sisters paid off, you're back on your feet Charlie," said Edna. "And you'll have all the casino money besides."

"I don't want that money. Bella deserves to reap the profits. We have lots of needs here, and with the growing tourist business, we'll have more."

Sheriff Schmidt grabbed Paddy's wrist and slipped one cuff on. "I'm arresting you for accessory, extortion, and a whole lot more. Dixie? I need to take you in, too." He put the other cuff on her and pulled the pair toward the door.

Dixie hesitated and looked back. "I'm so sorry, Charlie. I really am."

Charlie slid to the floor again, stupefied. "I've lost everyone. Two days, and everyone I care about—or used to care about—gone."

Ken started to say something, but then seemed to think better of it and just smiled at Charlie instead.

Edna slowly pulled herself up and walked over to the deflated young woman. "Charlie," she said, reaching down to take Charlie's hand. "Come with me into the kitchen."

Charlie looked up at her with a drained expression. Edna smiled.

"I have something to tell you."

Carolyn Lieberg's most recent book is called Little Sisters; *her previous book was* Calling The Midwest Home. *She formerly edited* Iowa Woman *and* The Goldfinch *(as Carolyn Hardesty) and now works at the Center for Teaching at the University of Iowa. She has two grown daughters, Adria and Rachel, and lives with her husband Craig, stepson Given, and cats Oscar and Edna in Iowa City. It never occurred to her that she would ever write a scene with a car chase in it.*

Dr. Barbara Lounsberry is a native of Cedar Falls, Iowa and has attended UNI from elementary, at Price Lab, to an M.A.. She received her Ph.D. at the University of Iowa. She is a continuation of a tradition in literature from her parents. She began an interest in literature through journalism. Besides journalism, she teaches courses in Literary Non-Fiction, Modern Drama and 20th Century American Literature. She is currently working with the well-known author, Gay Talese, in an anthology of writers in the Non-Fiction Tradition.

Gary Kelley graduated from the University of Northern Iowa. His career began as a graphic designer and art director before turning to illustration in the mid 1970s. Since then Gary has won the Hamilton King Award from the Society of Illustrators for Best Illustration in 1992, the Ben Franklin Award from national Booksellers Assn. for Best Illustrated Youth Fiction (1993), and numerous gold and silver medals from the Society of Illustrators.

Clients include The New Yorker, Rolling Stone, Playboy, Time, Newsweek, GQ among others. Gary recently completed two 70-foot murals for the renovated Barnes & Noble store at 5th Ave. and 48th Street in New York City.

Amy Roach is a graphic designer at The University of Iowa where she designs award-winning alumni magazines and recruitment materials.

She and her husband live in Cedar Rapids with their three children who graciously allowed her access to their family Mac to complete this project.